Words About
The Tales of Fort Word, Texas

"...offers challenge and support for every kind of young reader."
Dr. Pat Pinsent, Senior Research Fellow, National Centre for Research in Children's Literature, Roehampton University, London, England

---

"...a masterful job of presenting important values in a language children can understand."
-Red Steagall, 2006 Poet Laureate of Texas, 2003 Inductee into Hall of Great Westerners

---

"...will enrich the lives of many children."
Dr. Robert Brooks, Faculty, Harvard Medical School

"Young readers who like the West will find pleasure in this fanciful story of a Western town, its comical human characters with funny names, and its talking animals, birds, and snakes, who face problems just like the rest of us."
Elmer Kelton, Award-winning Western Novelist

"Ms. Mac did an amazing job to create humorous and identifiable characters with a set of vocabulary words."
Jerry Young, The Texas Tale Rattler, A Storyteller Extraordinaire

---

"I loved the play on words and the sneaky way that Ms. Mac incorporated those higher level vocabulary words into the text."
Janie D. Lombardi, President, Texas State Reading Association

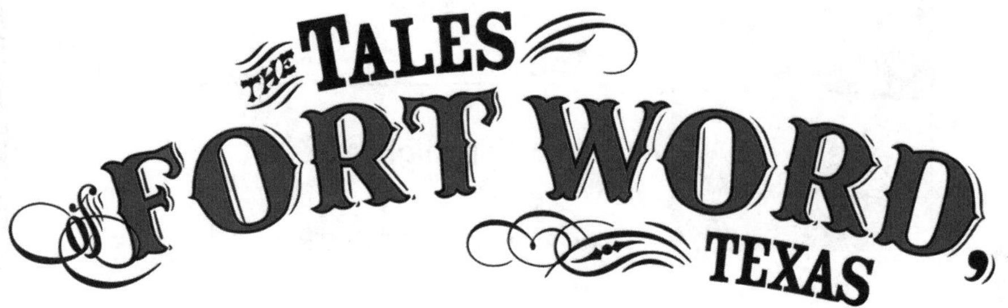

THE CONTEST

Written by Ms. Mac

Illustrated by Dan Foote

The Tales of Fort Word, Texas

Printed in the United States of America
Branch Smith Printing, Fort Worth, Texas

Library of Congress Catalog Card Number
2007902450

International Standard Book Number
978-0-9794147-01

Author: Ms Mac
Illustrator: Dan Foote
Editor: K. Celeste Seay
Cover Designer: Gina L. Miller

Publisher:

Mac Math Inc.
P. O. Box 70
Ballinger, Texas 76821
972-679-READ (7323)
www.fortword.com

We wish to extend our thanks

to all of our friends
young and old
new and seasoned
tried and true.

To God,
to our country,
and to our state,

we dedicate this book to you.

Ms. Mac and Dan Foote

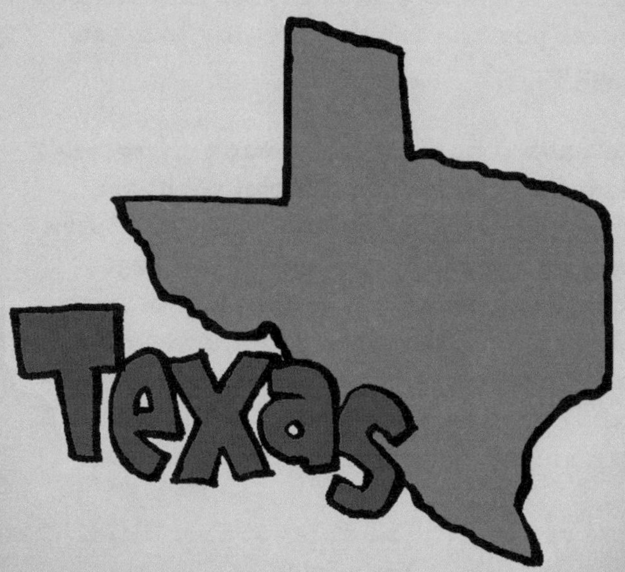

The Friendship State

To the Reader:

I wrote this book to entertain you while giving your brain a workout at the same time. The result should be greater mental efficiency. You know what I mean; you get more out of it for less work than you put into reading it.

Here's how: the special font, borders on the pages, and highlighted vocabulary allow your brain to focus its energy on understanding and remembering what you read. The more fun it is to read something, the easier it is to remember. The more you see something familiar, the stronger those neural pathways in your brain become. With the added humor and cartoon pictures you can laugh your way to a new vocabulary.

Take note: The meaning of each character's nickname is hidden in the picture at the beginning of each chapter. When you learn more about a character before you begin reading, the stronger a reader you become. In other words, the more you know, the easier it is to know more. The conundrums and memory challenge at the end of the book will help measure your mental improvement.

I hope you enjoy <u>The Tales of Fort Word, Texas</u>

Your friend,

Ms. Mac

msmac@fortword.com

Table of Contents

★THE CONTEST★

uncertain
Vacillating Vernon

multicolored
Variegated Verna

CHAPTER I

Perilous Pierre

IT MIGHT AS WELL BE SOONER

Private Pinnacle

Furtive Fernando

Clouds of dust spewed up. **Perilous** Pierre, the reckless and dangerous stagecoach driver for Roadrunner Express, pushed his team of horses past the fort and onto the flats outside of Fort Word, Texas. A buzzard perched on a nearby cactus coughed and spit out dust.

"Crazy no-good human! I don't care if he is carrying something important on that contraption. He's a pest and can hurt someone if he is not more careful."

Before the dusty interruption, **Furtive** Fernando, the secretive buzzard who was hidden in between the arms of a saguaro cactus, had been spying on **Vacillating** Vernon, a hesitant little rattlesnake. Vernon, with his mouth wide open, was gawking in awe at **Variegated** Verna, a breathtakingly colorful snake curled up ever so nicely under a nearby sagebrush.

Vernon could not make up his mind. Should he approach Verna? Should he ask her to be his friend? After all, she was something to look at; her skin was so unusual. It was covered with so many different colors and patterns.

"I'll ask her!" said Vernon to himself.

"Nope, I can't. She'll just say no," he argued.

"But if I don't ask her, I'll never find out. So I'll ask her!"

Uncertain

"I could wait until tomorrow," **vacillated** Vernon.

Then he took a deep breath and said, "No sirreee, I'd better do it today."

"Well, dadburn it! Can't you make up your mind?" yelled **Furtive** Fernando, whose voice immediately changed to a strong whisper, trying to be loud and secretive at the same time. Vernon looked up to see who was speaking and answered calmly.

"Oh, hi, Mr. Buzzard. Sorry about the distraction. But I always have trouble trying to make up my mind, and this is harder than usual. I don't know what to do to make a friendship stick. I want to try several things, but I'm not sure what to try first. Do I just come out and ask her, or do I bring her gifts? What makes it work?"

Fernando leaned closer and whispered, "If you won't tell anyone you saw, me, I'll tell you how to find out what to do. I have been watching you watch her, and it is a pretty sad situation."

Furtive Fernando pulled his hat lower over his eyes and his bandana higher up over his beak.

"What are you being so secretive about?" Vernon asked. "You're beginning to give me the creeps."

Fernando nodded his head

Uncertain

up toward the fort on the nearby hill.

"See that human? That's Private **Pinnacle** way up in the top of the tower, and that's a long rifle he's a carrying —and he has a hankering for shooting birds, " the buzzard said with a shiver. "I have to hide out until dark or at least until his gal walks by. He drools the same as you when it comes to those female types. Just a bit more dangerous to me though."

Furtive Fernando winked at Vernon as he continued. "If you want me to tell you about that friendship stuff, ask me anything. I know all about it. Spying has its benefits, you know."

"I would be much obliged for any assistance you can throw my way!" exclaimed **Vacillating** Vernon. "What do I have to do?"

Furtive Fernando crouched a little closer, nodded in the opposite direction and whispered,

"The answer to your question lies down yonder in the human town. I suggest that you begin at the general store. Things always seem to be stirring around there. Be careful though. Humans have a mighty strong dislike for slithering creatures. Those long rifles are everywhere."

"Who or what am I looking for?" asked **Vacillating**

Secretive

Vernon, trying to decide whether or not to go with the suggestions from this sneaky feather duster.

"You must look at everything and everyone closely," answered Fernando. "You'll know a friendship when you see it. Someone will definitely show you the answer. But, like I said, you need to be careful. I suggest you crawl under the boardwalk and steps. The space is too small for humankind, and it is a bit cooler."

Vacillating Vernon glanced back at **Variegated** Verna from the short distance. Ooooooh! She was so beautiful and so colorful. He looked back down at the human town, an awesome and dangerous place for sure. Vernon turned and looked at Fernando—then back at Verna—and finally he took a deep breath. **Vacillating** Vernon would have to make up his mind sooner or later.

He scrunched up his face in determination, swallowed hard, and started to crawl away.

"It might as well be sooner!" he said.

Roadrunner Express
FORT WORD
Texas

CHAPTER II

THERE

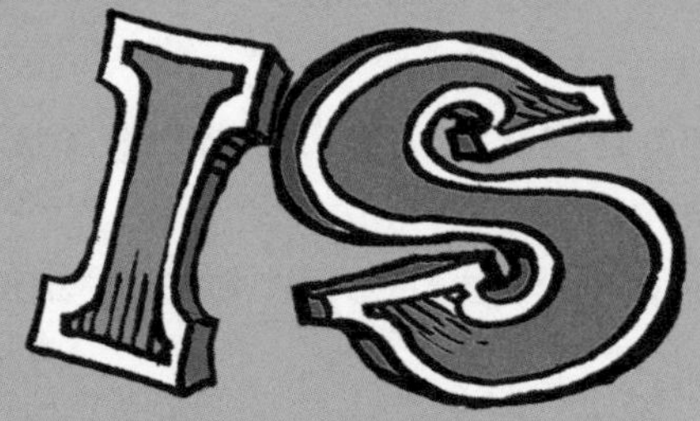

NOTHING LEFT, MA'AM

It was Monday morning. **Ethical** Ethelbert, the parson of the Peaceful Word Chapel, pulled the bell rope as hard and as fast as he could. It was the right thing to do. He had received the signal from Private **Pinnacle** at the top of the fort outside of town. He must warn the people with four loud rings of the church bell, warning to everyone to, "GET OFF THE STREETS!"

No one in the town or in the nearby countryside would mistake this warning. The fast clang-clang, clang-clang could not be confused with the twelve peals at noon that announce lunch or the soft rings on Sunday morning announcing the services at church.

No. Everyone understood that they had better clear off the main street of Fort Word, or their lives might be in danger. **Perilous** Pierre and the stagecoach, the Roadrunner Express, were on their way. The stagecoach had a reputation for speed, and **Perilous** Pierre was known for his reckless and dangerous driving.

From the distance, the billows of dust flying around the stagecoach looked like a tornado coming into town. If Pierre wasn't scheduled to pick up anyone, he didn't stop, even if he had a delivery. He would slow

Perilous Pierre

down just a bit at the corner, but that was it. Strangely enough, it was the love of his hat that placed him into the dangerous category. His tall ten-gallon hat, willed to him by his dear departed brother, was exactly three sizes too big. When he wore that hat—and that was all the time—he couldn't see a whole heck of a lot!

Depending on his horses to know the way, **Perilous** Pierre drove them through town hanging onto the reins with his teeth, another dangerous feat for a man who had only a few left in his mouth.

While biting down on the reins, **Perilous**

Pierre would lean back, reach out his hands and knock off the bundles and mailbag onto the ground. He timed his delivery perfectly as he rounded the corner at the end of town.

"Here he comes!" yelled a cowboy, running like the dickens.

Several men hurried out in anticipation. One was **Lavish** McTavish, the swanky and extravagant owner of the End-of-the-Trail Cattle Company. His business was next to the local newspaper office owned by an abrupt man, **Brevity** Bradford. Their buildings hugged the corner at the end of the main street in Fort Word. Both places would be in danger

Lavish McTavish

when the stagecoach made its turn.

Together, the men had placed a large stack of hay out in front of their buildings. This gave them protection as well as a soft cushion for **Perilous** Pierre's deliveries. The whole town watched in anticipation as the mail was delivered with a loud thud and as the horses were driven recklessly out of town.

"See y'all next week," shouted **Perilous** Pierre as his head and hat bobbed up and down.

"Hurry," urged **Brevity** Bradford, a man of few words. He pointed at the bundles to instruct his exhausted and overworked newsman, **Enervated** Ernie, to fetch the mail and bring it up onto the boardwalk.

"Caaaaaaaan't do it," responded Ernie in a tired voice.

Brevity Bradford looked closer. The mailbag lay on the ground next to a large wooden crate. The lid from the crate was broken and some of the contents had spilled out onto the hay.

"Unusual," observed **Brevity** Bradford as he picked up the lid and began to read the note attached to the outside of it. **Enervated** Ernie huffed and puffed as he tried to pull the damaged crate over to the boardwalk in front

EDITOR

Enervated Ernie

of the newspaper office.

People were drawn to the haystack. The stagecoach always caused people to scatter when it came through, but after it was gone, everyone would gather eagerly to see if they had received any mail.

As **Brevity** Bradford read the note silently, **Lavish** McTavish and his precise and fussy wife, **Scrupulous** Scarlett, and his overly obedient servant, **Servile** Nile, moved closer to the editor.

Doc **Salve** Salvador, a man of compassion, greeted the general store owner with a warm handshake.

"Expectin' somethin'?" Doc asked.

"Just more yard goods," answered **Replete** Pete, whose store was already crowded. "Can't have too many."

Prudent Prudence, the banker's wife, remained at the bank to watch the money while her husband, **Bountiful** Bogart, the generous president of the bank, went to check on his mail delivery.

Mercenary Mary, the money-grubbing saloon owner, stopped counting the money she received from the weekend gamblers and hurried to catch up with **Soporific** Sophie, the mesmerizing hotel owner. **Didactic** Dorothy, the

Didactic Dorothy

academic schoolmarm, let the children play outside the school as she hurried to see if her delivery of new books had arrived.

Since **Vexed** Tex, the frustrated blacksmith, and his soothing sweet wife, **Mollifying** Molly, lived on the edge of town, they were the last to arrive at the haystack.

News of the unusual delivery spread fast. Excitement was in the air! **Rectitude** Dude, the moral and upright sheriff, moseyed on out of Inmate Inn—his nickname for the jail—making sure that peace was maintained on the streets of his town. He gently pushed through the crowd seeking out newspaperman **Brevity** Bradford.

"What's up?" ask **Rectitude** Dude.

"Unbelieveable!" responded **Brevity** as he handed the note he was reading to the sheriff.

The broken crate revealed a number of wooden letters, some of which had fallen out onto the ground.

"That must be for the school," complained **Mercenary** Mary, disappointed that it wasn't something to help her make more money.

"Wait a minute, everyone!" shouted the sheriff. "You ALL might find this quite interesting."

People stood quietly as the sheriff began to read.

"TO THE GOOD PEOPLE OF FORT WORD, TEXAS:

Mercenary Mary

YOUR TOWN HAS BEEN HERE FOR MORE THAN TEN YEARS. YOU STARTED OUT AS A SMALL TENT CITY BENEATH THE SHADOW OF THE FORT. NOW THINGS HAVE CHANGED. THE DISCOVERY OF GOLD AND THE CATTLE BOOM HAVE MADE THIS TOWN A THRIVING COMMUNITY. YOU DESERVE AN AWARD. IF YOU CAN COME UP WITH THE WORD THAT BEST DESCRIBES THE TOWN, YOU WILL HAVE FOUND THE MOST VALUABLE THING THIS COMMUNITY HAS TO OFFER.

IF YOU CAN DETERMINE THE MOST VALUABLE WORD FOR FORT

WORD, TEXAS," [the sheriff paused and took a deep breath], "YOU WIN! EVERY BUSINESS HAS A CHANCE TO COME UP WITH THE ANSWER. THE CLUES ARE IN THE CRATE!"

With excitement beginning to take control of the crowd, the sheriff directed **Servile** Nile and **Envervated** Ernie to unload the contents of the crate.

Nile pulled out colorful blocks of wood, each about 12 inches high, carved into a letter of the alphabet.

Attached to each letter was a tag. On each tag was the name of one of the businesses in Fort Word, Texas.

Rectitude Dude

"Finish reading," **Brevity** Bradford reminded **Rectitude** Dude.

"Oh! yeah! Let me see. Here it is, uh; 'THE CLUES ARE IN THE CRATE. THE LETTER GIVEN TO YOUR BUSINESS WILL GUIDE YOU IN YOUR DECISION. YOU HAVE ONE WEEK TO DETERMINE WHICH WORD YOU BELIEVE TO BE THE SOLUTION. ONCE THAT DECISION IS MADE, YOUR WOODEN LETTER MUST BE HUNG FROM A HIGH POINT ON YOUR BUILDING. THIS LETS EVERYONE KNOW THAT YOU ARE READY FOR THE PRIZE. REMEMBER, IT IS TO BE A VALUABLE QUALITY NECESSARY FOR

THE CONTINUED SUCCESS OF FORT WORD, TEXAS. THE STAGECOACH WILL RETURN IN ONE WEEK TO DETERMINE A WINNER AND TO AWARD THE PRIZE.

GOOD LUCK!

(signed)

ONE WHO KNOWS' "

Enervated Ernie, as tired as he was, handed each letter to the sheriff, and he, in turn, read out the names on each tag.

" 'TO THE DOCTOR'S OFFICE,' Doc **Salve** Salvador, it looks like you get the big letter {D}," said the sheriff.

" TO THE SALOON,"

he continued,

Doc Salve Salvador

"**Mercenary** Mary, your group gets the letter {S}."

"I plan to make a lot of money from this," she responded.

" 'TO THE INVESTMENT BANK,' **Bountiful** Bogart, your letter is the letter {I}," announced **Rectitude** Dude.

Bogart smiled as he took the letter, "Looks like this is a new investment I never thought of!"

The sheriff nodded and continued.

" 'TO THE SADDLES AND SPURS STABLES,' **Vexed** Tex and Molly, it looks like a {S} for you."

" 'TO THE NEWSPAPER OFFICE,' **Brevity** Bradford, the letter {N}!"

"A newspaper letter!" smiled **Brevity** as he

took the piece of wood.

" 'TO INMATE INN, THE JAIL,' " **Rectitude** hesitated for a moment and then continued, "That's mine, and it looks like I get the letter {I}."

" 'TO HEAVENLY-HAVEN HOTEL.' **Soporific** Sophie, you get the letter {H}."

" 'TO THE END-OF-THE-TRAIL CATTLE COMPANY.' Mr. Mc Tavish, it looks like the letter {E} is for your business."

"An elegant letter, if I do say so myself," **Lavish** McTavish boasted.

" 'TO PEACEFUL WORD CHAPEL.' Parson **Ethical** Ethelbert, your church gets

Ethical Ethelbert

the letter {P}."

Enervated Ernie handed **Rectitude** Dude the last letter he found.

The sheriff read, " '**REPLETE** PETE'S GENERAL STORE.' **Replete** Pete, here is your letter {R}."

"This is more than enough," responded Pete with a smile as he took the letter.

Brevity Bradford helped **Servile** Nile pick up the broken pieces of the crate, turned to the crowd and, with only a few words, announced the end.

"That's all!" he shouted.

"Wait!" yelled Miss **Didactic** Dorothy, the schoolmarm. "I am the only one who didn't get anything. Isn't there a letter for the schoolhouse?"

Servile Nile once more looked carefully among the pieces of the crate. He slowly shook his head and answered, "I'm sorry. There's nothing left, ma'am."

CATTLE CO.
JAIL
STORE
SCHOOL

SALOON
DOC
HOTEL
BANK
CHURCH
STABLES

brief
Chief Concise Cochise

CHAPTER

III

to waste
Squander Squaw

filled
Replete Pete

EGGZZZZACTLY WHAT I WANTED

It was cool under the boardwalk, just as **Furtive** Fernando said it would be. Earlier that morning, **Vacillating** Vernon had cautiously slithered past the First Frontier Schoolhouse until he arrived outside of **Replete** Pete's Complete General Store. Excited about the possibilities, **Vacillating** Vernon could not make up his mind whether to climb out at the end of the walk or to stick his head up through the empty knothole he found. He heard a clop, clop, clop and then a big thud, as if something had been dropped on the floor above him. Vernon edged his head slowly up through the hole.

The first human **Vacillating** Vernon spotted was Chief **Concise** Cochise, a man whose words, although few, were always full of wisdom. As he was settling down in front of the store, the chief handed a pouch of beads to his daughter, **Squander** Squaw. Earlier that day, the elders of the tribe who lived near Fort Word, had expressed their concern that the young Indian maiden was again frittering away her collections of skins and beads on nothing more than books.

Squander Squaw did not argue with the name given to her, but down deep she knew that she was not squandering her beads or wasting her skins. She knew that she was finding

Brief

treasures in those books.

As **Squander** Squaw walked into **Replete** Pete's Complete General Store with reading on her mind, **Vacillating** Vernon's eyes followed her. Looking into the dark store, he could see only outlines of piles and piles of things. Then he saw the dark outline of a person speaking to the Indian maiden.

"That must be the owner, **Replete** Pete," he said to himself.

In Pete's hand was a wooden object. It was the letter {R} given to him by the sheriff the day before. **Replete** Pete was determined to win the the contest and was asking **Squander** Squaw, an obviously well-read person, for her opinion on his possible selections.

"Finding the most valuable word is going to be easy because I have more than enough words that begin with the letter {R} to choose from," he said. "There are many valuable things in the West that begin with the letter {R}. 'Roads' begin with the letter {R}; we can't get anywhere without a road. 'River' also begins with the letter {R}, and we have to have water to survive."

"What about 'rain'?" questioned **Squander** Squaw. "It starts with {R} and brings water, too."

Replete Pete looked around his store and saw

To waste

the numerous items he had to sell.

"This town sure has a lot of things," he said. "We are rich in many ways, so the predictable choice I guess would be 'riches'."

"Then that's your word," said **Squander** Squaw. "I'll get the chief to help you hang the letter if you have made your final decision, Pete," she said, tucking the newly purchased books, her own riches, under her arms.

Replete Pete was just about to reveal a different word, a special word, when a noise came from the street. It distracted Vernon, **Replete** Pete, **Squander** Squaw and everyone else close by.

A wagon pulled in front of the store. It was exciting for **Replete** Pete because it was overflowing with chicken crates, chickens, and baskets of eggs.

Rustic Rusty, a country chicken farmer and his wife, **Profuse** Priscilla, were bringing their over-abundant produce to sell at the store. Sitting in back of the wagon was their daughter, **Listless** Leslie. She was tired from the combination of rising early in the morning and then having to ride all the way to town with a wagon full of squawking birds.

Profuse Priscilla, sitting on the front seat of the wagon, was wearing a large apron with

Overflowing

numerous pockets. Each pocket was overflowing with eggs. On her lap were two baskets, one held one-half dozen of the finest brown eggs she had ever seen. The second basket held only one egg, the prize egg, which was large and colorful. Hoping to fetch a lot of money for such an unusual egg, she guarded it carefully.

Dressed for country work in his torn overalls and frayed straw hat, **Rustic** Rusty helped his wife down from the wagon. He turned to hand a chicken cage to **Listless** Leslie, giving her instructions to place it on the boardwalk in front of the store.

"I am so tired, and school will start soon,"

complained **Listless** Leslie.

"You have time to unload the wagon before going over to the schoolhouse," said **Rustic** Rusty to his daughter. "Just be careful."

Vacillating Vernon's head was bobbing up and down through the hole in the boardwalk. He was trying to make up his mind where to go. People were moving around, and it was all very exciting. He was looking for the answer to his question about **Variegated** Verna. **Furtive** Fernando had told him to look at everything and everybody.

Then their eyes met. **Vacillating** Vernon, mesmerized by the stare from

Country

Chief **Concise** Cochise, was getting a message loud and clear! The chief usually used very few words to communicate and now words were not even necessary. The snake and the Indian chief stared for what seemed like an eternity. At least that is what Vernon thought. He felt a shiver go through his body. Then the rattle at the end of his tail caught that shiver and rattled liked it had never rattled before.

Now, it is a known fact to anyone west of the Mississippi that chickens just plain hate snakes. That's a fact to take to the grave. Chickens just plain go berserk when they are close to a snake!

And **Rustic** Rusty's chickens were no different. They began flapping their wings and squawking. Surprised, **Listless** Leslie dropped the crate of chickens she was toting. Loose chickens and loose feathers flew everywhere. As **Profuse** Priscilla tried to move away from the ruckus, her shoe accidently hit the side of Vernon's head!

Profuse Priscilla lost her balance. She fell back. The basket with the brown eggs flew up into the air. The eggs in her apron were slung in every which direction. And the special basket with the special prize egg—it plopped to the floor and fell over.

Chief **Concise** Cochise finally spoke with an "Uhn," as

Country

an egg hit him in the face.

Splat! Splat! Splat!

Rustic Rusty, **Profuse** Priscilla, **Squander** Squaw, **Listless** Leslie and **Replete** Pete were all caught under the rain of eggs falling down on them.

Egg yolks and flying feathers were everywhere and on everyone! Humans began to look like chickens, and the chickens began to look like well, they looked like

NAKED CHICKENS!

"A reptile!" yelled Leslie as she spotted **Vacillating** Vernon, whose surprised eyes were still crossed from being hit.

Everyone stood still and stared. Their jaws

dropped. **Vacillating** Vernon wanted to tell them that the word 'reptile' starts with the letter {R}, but he knew that this was not the appropriate time.

Then, as if someone yelled, "GO," everyone bent over and found the nearest unbroken egg, picked it up and aimed it at **Vacillating** Vernon. For once in his life, Vernon rapidly made up his mind and decided to get out of there. He quickly pulled his head back through the hole in the boardwalk. He heard the thumping of the eggs as they broke on the boards above him. Then a soft rumbling noise caught his attention, and he saw something he did not

Uncertain

expect to come through the hole after him. It was the prize egg! Vernon wiped off this unique treasure, wrapped his tail around the egg, and crawled away into the cool darkness under the boardwalk.

"Friendships are sure messy at this place. But I know **Variegated** Verna will certainly be impressed," said Vernon as he gently nudged the egg.

"This is egggzzzactly what I needed!"

R
R

CHAPTER

IV

NEWS FLASH: HUMAN CREATURES ARE SO WEIRD!

quick
New News Newspaper
Expeditious Ezra

EDITOR
tired
Enervated Ernie

Vacillating Vernon dragged the prize egg under the boardwalk until he was tired. He didn't want to lose what he considered to be a special gift for **Variegated** Verna. He had to hide the egg somewhere until he finished his business in the human town.

Vacillating Vernon could not make up his mind about where a safe place might be. He crawled under the boardwalks and porches, past the jail, and up to the front of the End-of-the-Trail Cattle Company. He could go no farther. He was plain tuckered out. When he stopped to rest, he noticed that straw was piled along the edge of the boardwalk, making the space darker and cooler. Vernon reasoned that if he placed the egg under the straw, it would be safe and cool at the same time.

His head still hurt from **Profuse** Priscilla's shoe. He needed a rest. So Vernon curled up and was just falling asleep when he heard the clump, clump, clump of heavy footsteps above him on the boardwalk.

Vacillating Vernon looked up through the cracks and noticed a young man carrying a sack on his back. He was in a hurry. And the door from the New News Newspaper Office was left wide open.

"Faster, faster," yelled the concise editor,

Overflowing

Brevity Bradford, with his usual short instructions.

Brevity Bradford sent **Expeditious** Ezra to deliver the newspaper around town. It was a one-page edition that described the contest, the rules and the possible prize for the winner. **Expeditious** Ezra was the fastest boy in Fort Word. His long legs and his skinny body made him look like a roadrunner. Ezra had even collected several roadrunner feathers to put in the band of his hat. He hadn't seen any of the birds lately and wondered why the roadrunners had disappeared from the area.

Vacillating Vernon slithered through the

door of the newspaper office while **Brevity** Bradford watched Ezra running quickly down the street. Vernon, looking for a hiding spot, crawled under a huge pile of crumpled papers next to a large desk.

"Ca-chunk, Ca-chunk. Ca-chunk, Ca-chunk!"

Vernon stuck his head out from under the papers to see what the noise was. **Enervated** Ernie, with drooping head and slumped body, was running the printing press. He was exhausted from staying up all night setting the type. Now he was printing the last copies that needed to be finished before **Expeditious** Ezra returned for his second delivery.

Quick

"Ohhhhhhhhh!" moaned Ernie, "I don't know when I have been more tired."

Brevity Bradford walked back into the building, sat down at his desk, and picked up his quill pen. He dipped the end into the inkwell and signed his name to the papers in front of him.

"Finished?" the editor asked his employee, laying his pen down on the desk.

"I need only three dozen more for the Fort," **Enervated** Ernie responded with a deep sigh.

"Tired?" asked **Brevity** Bradford.

Enervated Ernie sat down in the chair next to the editor's desk.

"I need to rest a bit before the last

printing," he said.

"Five minutes," reminded **Brevity** Bradford as he, too, took a break, leaning back in his chair and putting his feet up on the desk. He picked up the letter {N} that the sheriff had given him for his clue.

"Hmmmm," he said as he ran his hand up and down the letter. **Brevity** Bradford pushed back his visor to take a closer look at the way the letter was put together.

"Have you made up your mind about the word you are going to enter in the contest?" continued Ernie.

"Yep!" answered **Brevity**.

"You fixin' to hang up the

Shortened

letter?" continued Ernie.

"Yep!" repeated **Brevity** Bradford.

"Need my help?" **Enervated** Ernie moaned, wondering if he was going to be able to finish his work by the end of the day.

"Yep!" **Brevity** Bradford said as he smiled. He was sure that the word he picked that began with {N} had a good chance to win.

"Well, let me lay my head down for just a few minutes, then I will finish the printing and help you hang the letter on the eaves of the roof," he said.

Worn out, **Enervated** Ernie was glad to have a rest. He placed his hand and arm down on the edge of the desk to use as a pillow. Too tired to notice, Ernie pushed the feather pen to the edge of the desk and knocked it off.

"No!" shouted **Brevity** Bradford as he tried to catch the quill pen falling from the desk into the pile of discarded papers.

Brevity Bradford and **Enervated** Ernie got down on their hands and knees and searched through the mess on the floor.

"Important! Antique! Quill pen!" **Brevity** Bradford gasped in his brief description to **Enervated** Ernie who quickly became tired of digging through trash.

Vacillating Vernon felt something ticklish on his

Shortened

backside. He gently curled his tail around it and pulled it closer to his eyes. He was pleasantly surprised to see a feather with a dark metal tip. It made him think of **Variegated** Verna who wore a feather in her headband. Vernon smiled because he knew that this item would make her happy. He decided to thank the nice human for such a wonderful gift just about the same time that **Brevity** Bradford unsuspectingly grabbed ahold of Vernon's mid-section and yanked him up through the papers.

"AAAAAAAAAAAAAAAAAAAAAAAAAAAAAAAAAAAAAAAAAAAHHHHHHHHHHHHHHHHHHHHHHHHH!" screamed **Brevity** Bradford, realizing what he had in his hand, that scream being the longest expression to ever leave his lips.

Enervated Ernie surprised himself, too. He quickly reacted to seeing **Vacillating** Vernon and to hearing his editor's scream. He moved like a bolt of lightning. Before he knew it, he was on top of the desk jumping up and down.

The editor, scared and shaking, dropped Vernon and jumped onto the desk next to Ernie. Clinging to each other, the two newsmen grabbed what they could off the desk and started throwing things at a very surprised snake.

"Out!" screamed **Brevity** Bradford.

Stunned at first, Vernon

Shortened

realized that he was still holding on to the quill pen. He shook his head and quickly beat a path out of the front of the office and slithered back under the boardwalk.

Vacillating Vernon placed the quill pen next to his prize egg in the hay. He took a deep breath and curled up thinking about the nap he needed.

"Here's a news flash. Those human creatures are so weird," mumbled **Vacillating** Vernon to himself as he drifted off to sleep.

"They are supposed to be friendly, but all they seem interested in is yelling and zzzzzzzzzzzz throwing things ... zzzzzzzzzzz."

N
INK
EDITOR
New News
Newspaper

CHAPTER

EASY WITHDRAWAL FROM A BANK

Plentiful

It was a cool Wednesday morning when **Bountiful** Bogart and his wife, **Prudent** Prudence, opened the front door to the bank. They were met by the well-mannered and respectful bank clerk, **Humble** Trumble.

"Good morning sir, ma'am," he said as he tipped his clerk's cap.

"Good morning, Trumble," responded **Bountiful** Bogart. "This day is going to be filled with many good things. I can feel it in my bones."

Bogart, the investment bank owner, wanted everyone to have more than enough. So he worked hard, to not only protect the money and gold that people brought to him, but to make it grow. **Prudent** Prudence, just as dedicated as her husband, was very careful to record the correct amounts on the bank books. She saw that they were always in order and exact.

From across the street, **Vacillating** Vernon watched the couple enter the bank. He argued with himself as to how safe it was to cross the street. He could see that a long boardwalk extended from Heavenly Haven Hotel on the corner all the way down to the Saddles and Spurs Stables at the other end of the street. The bank, next to the hotel, was right in the middle.

"If I can just make it across without someone stepping on me, I'll be safer than

Sensible

money in the bank," Vernon said to himself, laughing at his own wit.

Vernon looked back at his prize egg and his feather pen. Covering them with extra hay, he felt that they would be safe while he was gone. He squeezed out from under the boardwalk and wiggled through the haystack at the end of the street.

He was just about to make his move to cross the street when he heard a loud "Yaaah-hoooo!"

Coming into Fort Word was a short hairy man wearing dusty clothes. His face was outlined in a red curly beard and his head was covered with a crumpled hat. He was leading the strangest-looking mule Vernon had ever seen.

Bountiful Bogart, **Prudent** Prudence, and **Humble** Trumble stepped out on the boardwalk.

"Yaaah-hooo!" again yelled the old prospector, **Fortuitous** Louis, as he tied up **Rotund** Ruby to the hitching post in front of the Bank. "I am so lucky! I am so lucky! I hit the big lode, and it's all because of my jewel of a mule, Ruby."

Vacillating Vernon looked carefully at Ruby. She was a mule all right, but it was hard to tell because she was wearing a bucket for a hat. And her walk was more like a waddle because she was as round as she was tall. Even though Ruby was carrying a mountain of bags and gear,

Modest

she was one heck of a large, round four-legged animal all by herself.

With everyone's attention directed toward the miner and his mule, Vernon used that exact moment to move quickly from the haystack to cross the dirt street and to crawl under the boardwalk in front of the hotel. From there he easily made his way to the bank. **Vacillating** Vernon listened carefully to the excited human.

"I've got gold to invest, Bogart!" exclaimed **Fortuitous** Louis. "I've got gold to invest!"

"How did you get so much gold?" asked **Bountiful** Bogart, as took the bags from the lucky gold miner and handed them to **Humble**

Trumble to carry inside.

"Be careful," **Prudent** Prudence said. "We don't want to spill any of this."

The miner nodded his head in agreement and began telling the exciting account of his discovery.

"Well, my Ruby and my lucky silver coin are reasons I am here. I found all of this gold just because I dropped my lucky silver coin," answered **Fortuitous** Louis. "Ruby stepped on top of it, and when I tried to get her to back up, she got spooked and started kicking with her hind legs. We were in Crooked Canyon where my claim is staked out. Ruby was so closed-in that, when she kicked, her hooves hit the

side of the canyon wall. And that is how I discovered the gold nuggets underneath!"

Fortuitous Louis retold his story several times as the four humans continued to unload the bags of gold from Ruby and carry them into the bank.

Vernon used the commotion as an opportunity to come up from under the boardwalk and through the doorway. Once he moved inside, Vernon realized that there wasn't a safe place to hide. Then he spotted a small opening between the sacks of gold on the floor. He crawled in between them and listened. More bags were piled on until the last one was firmly placed on the top by Louis.

"Twenty bags!" he exclaimed as he slapped the pile. "I dug for fourteen days and nights, and here I am. Twenty bags of gold, my favorite friend, **Rotund** Ruby, and my lu-ucky silver coin," said **Fortuitous** Louis as he held up the coin for everyone to see.

Vacillating Vernon poked his head out from his hiding place and looked up at the coin. He could tell that **Fortuitous** Louis was prouder of that one piece of money than he was of all his gold.

"I am giving each of you a bag of gold for being my friend and supporter," exclaimed Louis.

"Thank you sir, but

Fat

I do not deserve it, Mr. Louis," responded **Humble** Trumble. "I just do the odd jobs around here. I know nothing about investing."

"Everyone has a purpose, Trumble, and you have always been nice to me. I am lucky to know you," said **Fortuitous** Louis as he unknowingly laid the silver coin close to where Vernon was hiding. He picked up a bag.

"So here, take this bag of gold, and do what you think is right."

Humble Trumble nodded his head in respect and took the bag. **Fortuitous** Louis handed one bag to Bogart and one to Prudence.

"I will invest this wisely," said **Bountiful**

Bogart, "and it will multiply, I promise."

"You do what you think is best," replied Louis.

Prudent Prudence nodded. "And I will not waste an ounce of it either, Mr. Louis."

Bountiful Bogart, **Prudent** Prudence, **Humble** Trumble and **Fortuitous** Louis walked over to the desk to complete the paperwork that was needed for the deposit.

Vernon was encouraged. He like this sharing thing. It made everyone's voice calmer and sweeter. Then as Vernon looked up, he spotted the silver coin.

"Well, isn't this nice. I guess he wants to share his luck with me," thought Vernon.

Plentiful

"If one shiny silver coin can make a person, a human person , become so generous and kind and friendly, then it must be special."

Vernon left the bank unnoticed, the coin firmly in his mouth. He was excited about sharing it with **Variegated** Verna and pleasantly surprised at how easy it was to make deposits and withdrawals from a bank!

TELLER

CHAPTER VI

drowsy
Heavenly Haven Hotel
Soporific Sophie

quiet
Serene Maureen

not enough
Meager Meagan

I AM ALWAYS IN HOT WATER!

General **Garrulous** Garrison walked through the front doors of the Heavenly Haven Hotel. He talked constantly and allowed for very little interruption. Oddly, he was seeking a quiet, peaceful place for his quiet, peaceful daughter, **Serene** Maureen. She had just arrived at Fort Word, Texas, under army escort.

General **Garrulous** Garrison explained to **Soporific** Sophie, the mesmerizing owner of hotel, why his daughter needed to stay in her establishment.

"My daughter can not stay at the Fort, Sophie, too much noise and commotion there. Now let me repeat myself, too much commotion.

Maureen likes peace and quiet. She has a gentle disposition and needs peaceful suroundings. Peaceful surroundings are what she needs," said the talkative general.

Meager Meagan, Sophie's poor gangly maid, who had arrived in Fort Word, Texas, the month before with the clothes on her back and a few belongings, smiled at **Serene** Maureen. It was nice to know that another young woman would be close by. She took the suitcases and led Maureen to her room. Looking back over her shoulder, she noticed that the general was still talking. He was being accompanied out of the hotel by Miss Sophie. If **Soporific** Sophie ever got a

Drowsy

chance to talk, she would surely begin one of her boring stories about past events in Fort Word. Sophie could put anyone to sleep, as her name implied, telling those stories. Meagan was sure that if the general did not return to the fort soon, he would be trapped into listening.

As the young ladies were walking down the hall, a loud voice came barreling out from behind one of the closed doors.

"MORE HOT WATER! I NEED MORE HOT WATER!" hollered **Laggard** Luke from his room.

Meager Meagan grimaced, knowing that she would have to tote more buckets of hot water up the stairs. Since **Slothful** Slim and **Laggard** Luke arrived, **Meager** Meagan had to wait on the two slow-moving, lazy cowboys constantly.

Meagan showed Maureen to her room and began her story about **Slothful** Slim.

"Wait till you see this guy," said Meagan. "His legs are so bowed that a stampeding herd of hungry dogies would have no trouble getting through them."

"What are dogies, and what made him that way?" asked **Serene** Maureen in her calm, soft voice.

"Dogies are what we call young cows, and well, well **Slothful** Slim is a cowboy, an extremely slow and lazy cowboy. He just sits up in

Slow

saddle most of the time. He lets his horse do all the work, and because he is so lazy, he doesn't even get off. The horse just slides right out from underneath him!" exclaimed Meagan.

Laughing, **Serene** Maureen knew that **Meager** Meagan was going to be a good friend.

"After you take care of the hot water for **Laggard** Luke, come back to my room. I have something to show you," said **Serene** Maureen.

Meager Meagan also sensed the beginning of a friendship. She did not own much, and it was obvious from all the suitcases that Maureen had so much more. But that would not matter.

Meagan opened the window to air out the

room and excused herself, hurrying to get the water for Luke.

Meanwhile, there was a commotion of sorts out in front of the hotel. **Soporific** Sophie was directing one of her hired hands to climb to the top of the front of the hotel to hang the letter {H}. This was the clue given to her on Monday for the contest. She had already decided what she considered to be the most valuable word, and she was ready to let everyone know it.

Vacillating Vernon was curled up under the boardwalk. He was looking closely at the lucky coin from the bank. He hoped that it would bring him luck. So far, he hadn't had much of

Drowsy

that in the human town. The sound of someone stomping around above his head began to remind him of the messy episode at **Replete** Pete's Complete General Store the day before. He knew he would have to keep on the move.

"No! Yes! Maybe," said **Vacillating** Vernon looking back and forth trying to make up his mind as to which direction to go. Then he heard a window open in the alley. A trellis covered in honeysuckle was attached to the western wall of the hotel. Hearing the soft voices of Meagan and Maureen, he decided to climb up the trellis and through the window instead of going through the front door. Slithering up the vines, he cautiously put his head on the sill of the window.

Inside, the two young women were discussing the piles of clothes on the bed and in all the suitcases that littered the room.

"I can help you with the unpacking now. I toted four buckets of hot water. That should keep **Laggard** Luke quiet," said **Meager** Meagan.

Serene Maureen sighed. "A little peace and quiet after such a long and noisy trip would help."

"You'll find it here at Heavenly Haven Hotel. Miss Sophie does all she can to make sure that everyone sleeps like an angel," responded **Meager** Meagan. "In fact, if you have trouble

Not Enough

going to sleep, all you have to do is ask Miss **Soporific** Sophie to tell you one of her tales about the guests who have stayed here before. Her stories start out exciting, but I guarantee you that they will end up putting you to sleep. And then only if she doesn't fall asleep first!"

The girls laughed and continued to talk while they tried on clothes. The main topic of discussion was Private **Pinnacle**, a young man in the highest tower at the fort who caught **Serene** Maureen's eye.

Hearing the soft laughter, Vernon was sure that this was the place to learn all about friendships. Maybe he could even learn what these female people were really like. He slipped into the room and hid under a bundle of soft clothes that were piled on the floor. Vernon was surprised by the sweet smell that accompanied the clothes. Closing his eyes, he took a deep breath, inhaling the wonderful aroma.

Vernon did not see **Serene** Maureen as she bent over and picked up a garment near his head. Alarmed and without thinking, Vernon's tail instinctively began to rattle.

"EEEEEK! A snake!" yelled one female person.

"EEEEEK! A snake!" yelled the other one.

Quiet

Screaming, the girls ran

out of the room and down the hall. Vernon was feeling bad about scaring them. He wanted to make amends and took off after the gals.

Hearing the bloodcurdling screams, **Laggard** Luke pulled himself out of the tub, wrapped a towel around himself, and peered out of his door. He stepped into the hall. When he spotted Vernon, he too screamed, dropped his towel, and ran down the hall in nothing but his birthday suit!

"SNAKE ON THE LOOSE! SNAKE ON THE LOOSE!" echoed throughout the hotel.

Luke's towel landed right on top of poor Vernon, and because he knew what usually follows the screaming, Vernon didn't **vacillate**. He quickly made his exit down the stairs and headed toward the front doors of the hotel. As he went through the lobby, Vernon observed the humans. **Laggard** Luke had jumped into the arms of his friend **Slothful** Slim who had just arrived. He noticed also that General **Garrulous** Garrison, who had returned to check on his daughter's accomodations, was holding **Soporific** Sophie who had jumped into *his* arms at the first warning of a snake. This was the only time that General **Garrulous** Garrison was at a loss for words. He was too surprised, too stunned, and too embarrassed.

Meager Meagan and **Serene** Maureen, who wondered if she

Not Enough

would ever find peace and quiet in this town, were clutching each other while balancing in a large upholstered chair.

"Friends here don't seem to be too heavy to carry around," concluded Vernon from his observations. "I wonder how much **Variegated** Verna weighs? Or is that something you don't ask a girl? I'll have to remember to check on that."

Dragging the towel, Vernon moved as quickly as possible out the front doors of Heavenly Haven Hotel.

"I am always in hot water," sighed **Vacillating** Vernon to himself, "And I haven't even had a bath! They call this heavenly?"

HHH
H
Heavenly
Haven
Hotel

CHAPTER VII

A GIANT LUMPY WORM!

It was Thursday morning, **Candid** Candace was standing in front of her pa's office. He was the only doctor for miles around, and she was proud of him. She was looking at the letter {D} hanging from the top of the building. Candace knew what word her father had selected for his entry in the contest. She had heard him use the word many times before and she knew how important it was to him.

Vacillating Vernon, sticking his head out from under the boardwalk, noticed Candace as he was trying to make up his mind where to go next. Seeing **Candid** Candace in front of the doctor's office made him think about females, Verna in particular. His mission to find the answer for capturing her heart was firm in his mind.

"Maybe a doctor will know what to do," Vernon said to himself as he moved under the boardwalk.

"If a doctor can fix those crazy humans, maybe he can fix my problem."

Stopping suddenly, **Vacillating** Vernon recoiled as he heard a coughing sound coming from a very ugly man headed towards the doctor's office.

It was **Deleterious** Delbert, an obviously very sick person who did not take good care of himself. He stumbled and coughed as he made his way up the steps.

"Shots hurt, mister," said Candace. "And if you don't do

Hurtful

things to stay healthy, you have to have shots!"

Candid Candace always told things as she saw them. She was honest and straightforward. But **Deleterious** Delbert did not feel any better by listening to her honest opinion. He hated shots and had put off coming to see the doc because he was flat scared of them.

"Got to get to school, mister," continued **Candid** Candace. "Pa's inside. Go on in!"

Seeing this as an opportunity, Vernon quickly and **furtively** slithered up onto the porch. His pal, Fernando, would be proud to see how sneaky he had become. When **Deleterious** Delbert opened the door to Doc **Salve** Salvador's office, Vernon slipped in unnoticed and hid behind the first piece of furniture he spotted.

"Have a seat, Delbert," said Doc **Salve** Salvador to his second patient of the day.

Known for his kindness and determination to help soothe the miseries of others, Doc Salvador turned to pay full attention to a patient already in the inner office.

Earlier in the week, **Stuporous** Stan, a local cowhand, had absent-mindedly stepped in front of some angry steers. Those cattle ran right over him. Poor **Stuporous** Stan. His leg was broken,and he had bruises from head to

Makes healthy

toe. Doc **Salve** Salvador had just finished tying the leg to a wooden splint and gave the injured cowpoke a crutch to help him walk.

However, it was Stan's mind that the doc was the most worried about. **Stuporous** Stan always seemed a little out of it, kind of confused and unsure of himself. Now, following the accident, his confusion had worsened, and he was complaining about forgetting stuff.

"These things just take time," Doc Salvador said. "Have a seat here in the waiting room and relax a few minutes more before you leave. Rest will do wonders. Staying out of the way of a stampede would be my other prescription. Soon, you will be able to think again and figure out all of your problems."

Doc **Salve** Salvador gently patted **Stuporous** Stan on his back. **Vacillating** Vernon was impressed. He liked the kind words that Doc Salvador shared. Vernon was beginning to feel comfortable with this human and wanted to learn more.

When Doc motioned for **Deleterious** Delbert to go into the inner office, Delbert started coughing and groaning. Following the doctor, he slowly walked into the next room.

Vacillating Vernon cautiously slipped in behind the two men and found a place to

Hurtful

Makes healthy

hide under a table.

"I kkkumph," he coughed, "noticed you hung your letter {D} outside your office," said **Deleterious** Delbert in a hoarse voice. "Have you already decided on the word you think is the most valuable?"

"Yes, I have," answered Doc **Salve** Salvador. "It's a word that made a deep impression on me at medical school back East. It truly is valuable, and this town could not survive without it."

Deleterious Delbert began to cough and wheeze as the doctor examined him.

"Well, you look and sound mighty poor," said the doctor. "Have you quit chewing that nasty awful tobacco?"

"Kkkuummph! Nope!" replied the ailing and now very embarrassed man.

"Well, have you quit drinking that demon whiskey?" asked Doc **Salve** Salvador.

"Naw," admitted Delbert. "And I haven't stopped using those stinky 'seegars' like you told me to either, Doc."

"Well, that presents a problem, Delbert. One that your body will have to pay dearly for," replied the doctor, trying to soothe his patient. Delbert hung his head, feeling miserable and ashamed.

"Your daughter, **Candid** Candace, said that I have to get a shot. Is that the honest

Truthful

truth?" asked the worried patient.

"I'm sorry to say yes. Your lungs have an infection, but a shot will take care of it. That's the good news. But," Doc **Salve** Salvador paused.

"But what, Doc?" asked **Deleterious** Delbert anxiously.

The doctor turned around and whispered, "It has to go into your, uhhh, your, uhhh, sitting-down part!"

"My rear end!" yelled Delbert. "I don't want it in my rear end!"

Doc **Salve** Salvador tried to soothe **Deleterious** Delbert by explaining each step.

First, he laid all the needles on a clean tray and showed the needles that could be used for the shot.

"Delbert, I will use the shortest and smallest needle! How about that? And when we are finished, you can pick out a piece of ribbon candy from the candy jar. In fact, that is why people nicknamed me '*Sweet Doc,*'" smiled the doctor.

Delbert, grumbling and coughing, seemed to accept his fate. He bent over and slowly dropped his trousers per Doc **Salve** Salvador's instructions.

Just at that moment, **Vacillating** Vernon, gaining confidence, moved closer. Catching the motion from the corner of his eye,

Makes healthy

the doctor turned and spotted Vernon. A snake was the last thing he expected to see.

"Oh my!" gasped the Doc. Shocked to see a snake in his office, he backed up quickly. Losing his balance, he bumped into the table holding the needles. His hand landed on the edge of the tray, flipping it over. All the needles—long, short, big and little were thrown up in the air.

Up went the needles. Down came the needles. Down, down, down, right into the—

"AAAAAAAAHHHHHHH!" screamed a very surprised **Deleterious** Delbert.

Vernon watched this sick man come alive with excitement. Delbert started running around the room with all the needles stuck in his—uh—where he didn't want them. Delbert swore some, and then said some more bad words, and then swore that he would give up his bad habits, if someone would

"JUST GET THEM OUT!"

Vernon's eyes widened at all the commotion. It was a sight to see—**Deleterious** Delbert, jumping around with needles sticking out his bottom, Doc **Salve** Salvador chasing after him, and both crashing into another table, the one with the candy jar on it.

It was just like the needles. Candy went up. Candy came down. Most of the pieces of

Makes healthy

Dazed

the sticky candy fell out and onto the floor. But several pieces of the ribbon candy stuck to **Vacillating** Vernon's back!

Stuporous Stan, who was sluggishly sitting in the waiting room as the doctor had instructed, noticed the noise in the back room. He sat up and, to his surprise, met the problem face-to-face. Stan reached to open the front door to escape.

But Vernon rushed past Stan, high-tailing it out of the doorway, scared, confused, and loaded down with sticky candy!

"Doc!" screamed **Stuporous** Stan as he hurried toward the backroom. "Help me! Help me! I'm—I'm seeing things! I—just—

I—just—I just—saw—

A GIANT LUMPY WORM!"

Leaving the noise behind, **Vacillating** Vernon was sliding on his belly as fast as he could. Moving quickly, he soon made his way back to the safety of the haystack. Vernon crawled under the boardwalk, wiggling left and right, rolling around until he felt the sticky candy fall off his back.

Vacillating Vernon took a closer look at the stuff that he had removed. He sniffed it, and then his forked tongue gently touched it.

"Yum! I wonder if it is correct and proper to offer a lady something as sweet as this?" Vernon asked himself, wishing he

Uncertain

had someone wise to ask. Then, as if by magic, his wish was granted. A traveler on horseback rode by.

"Clip-Clop! Clip-Clop! Clip-Clop!"

Vernon stuck his head out from under the hay to look in the direction of the noise. He smiled. **Vacillating** Vernon didn't **vacillate** this time. He left the candy with the other treasures and followed the passing sound of the horse's hooves.

CHAPTER VIII

JUSTICE AT INMATE INN

His Honor, **Venerable** Vin Ho, dismounted his horse in front of Inmate Inn, the nickname given to the only jail for miles around. The circuit judge was well respected in these parts, partially because of his age; he was very old, and partially because of the dignity he brought to the law.

Rectitude Dude, the sheriff, had written to the judge concerning the inmates of Inmate Inn. Always trying to do what was correct and right, the sheriff needed a decision about how long he could keep the bad guys locked up.

There were three residents in the jail, but only one was a real criminal. His name was **Infamous** Amos, and he had a bad reputation far and wide. He was mean, nasty and downright ornery. **Infamous** Amos had robbed more banks and stagecoaches than any other outlaw in the Old West. He was a nasty bully, and he loved to scare everyone, especially little old ladies.

After robbing them of their money and jewelry, Amos would make every sweet little lady who crossed his path take off her hat and place it on the ground so he could crush it under his boots. No one felt good about **Infamous** Amos, and now that he had been caught, most people wanted justice.

The people of Fort Word, Texas, looked up to **Venerable** Vin Ho for wisdom and

knowledge. The judge knew what the law said, and he knew how to be fair. His long robe and long beard made him look distinguished. His appearance also gained the respectful attention of **Vacillating** Vernon, who had managed to hide behind a barrel next to the jail.

"A wise judge would know what to do about Verna," **Vacillating** Vernon thought. "This has got to be the place to find the answer."

Suddenly, an extremely loud noise boomed from the barred window above his head. Vernon changed his mind about trying to get through the front door and decided that he could climb up on top of the barrel and check things out from the window ledge. Being safe had become a priority to Vernon when it came to dealing with human noises.

The cautious snake squinted his eyes as he peered inside the jail cell. Two funny-looking cowpokes were moving around making all kinds of noises.

"IT HURTS! IT HURTS! IT HURTS!" yelled **Vociferous** Virgil, directing his attention to his cellmate. "AND BECAUSE OF YOU WE ARE STUCK IN THIS HORRIBLE JAIL!"

Raucous Rowdy Roddy responded with a louder voice, "YOU GOT IN MY WAY. IT WASN'T MY FAULT! IT IS YOUR FAULT WE ARE STUCK IN THIS HORRIBLE JAIL!"

Shouting

Loud

Vernon listened to the two extremely loud cowhands talk about the accident.

The problem started when **Raucous** Rowdy Roddy, while carelessly playing around with a bow and arrow, shot **Vociferous** Virgil in his left foot. **Vociferous** Virgil screamed, which is not unreasonable, except that his screechy voice could turn a person's blood cold. **Raucous** Rowdy Roddy tried to cover up **Vociferous** Virgil's yelling because he knew that he would get in trouble for shooting that bow and arrow in town. But then he forgot he would get into trouble for shooting guns in town. **Raucous** Rowdy Roddy grabbed his six-shooters and fired them into the air: "KER-BANG! KER-BANG! KER-BANG! KER-BANG!"

When all the noises that **Vociferous** Virgil and **Raucous** Rowdy Roddy were making reached the ears of the sheriff, **Rectitude** Dude quickly arrested the two for disturbing the peace and put them in a jail cell. They had been residents of Inmate Inn for more than a week, arguing day after day with each other.

Now that **Venerable** Vin Ho had arrived, things would be different. The sheriff was sure about that.

Vociferous Virgil and **Raucous** Rowdy Roddy quieted down when **Rectitude** Dude

Goodness

shook hands with the judge.

"Judge," **Rectitude** Dude said, "it is an honor to have such a wise person here in our town to pass judgment on these guys. But before you hold court, do you think you could help me with this?"

The sheriff handed the wooden letter {I} the judge.

"I heard about the contest," responded **Venerable** Vin Ho. "Word gets around. What would you like for me to do? Help you hang it up?

"Well, not quite," said **Rectitude** Dude. "I want to do what is right. I have come up with several good words that begin with the letter {I}. It's just that I'm not too sure which one is the wisest choice.

"The wisest choice, Sheriff, is the one that is closest to the heart," answered **Venerable** Vin Ho. "You are full of moral goodness. Go with your gut feeling and the choice will be the right one."

The sheriff thanked the judge for his advice. He instantly knew which word he would choose. **Rectitude** Dude then began telling **Venerable** Vin Ho about the residents of Inmate Inn.

Vociferous Virgil and **Raucous** Rowdy Roddy listened as the sheriff told the judge about their problem.

"Bring them to me," ordered the judge.

Rectitude Dude opened

Honored  the cell door and told the two young hoodlums to stand in front of the desk where **Venerable** Vin Ho was ready to pass his sentence.

"I'll tell you what," said the judge. "Disturbing the peace does not seem important to some people, but because we need to live peacefully together, it is important to me."

The two loud-mouths, for once, did not mutter a sound.

"I am ready to pass judgment," continued the judge. "It is obvious that the hardest thing for you to do is to be quiet. So I will make a deal with you. If you are able to stay perfectly quiet for one hour, I will allow the sheriff to release you. But you can not utter a word! You have to learn to control yourselves, to get along with each other, and to do it in a peaceful manner. If you say one word, I have no choice but to make your stay in Inmate Inn last a long time."

Vociferous Virgil and **Raucous** Rowdy Roddy anxiously nodded their heads. One hour did not seem difficult. In fact, it would be like taking candy from a baby!

"Why can't I have the same?" demanded **Infamous** Amos, calling from his cell.

"Your time is coming," replied the sheriff. "Just wait your turn."

Now, **Vacillating** Vernon, watching from the window,

Rotten

was sure that this was a place where he could learn something. He dropped down onto the bed against the window and quickly slipped underneath.

Rectitude Dude put the two jailbirds back into their cell and asked if they wanted to say something before their 'hour of quiet' began.

"Just begin the clock," said Roddy.

"We're ready to go," said **Vociferous** Virgil.

"Fine," said the sheriff as he locked the door. He turned to walk back to visit with the judge about the remaining inmate, the real criminal, the one with the bad reputation.

Once the sheriff had left, Amos started in

on the two quiet cowpokes.

"I think you are nothing but a bunch of sissies!" teased **Infamous** Amos, trying to get Virgil and Roddy upset enough to break their silence.

Infamous Amos was determined to mess up the judge's whole plan. He loved to make people miserable. He knew that his stay in jail would probably be for a long time. He might as well make sure everyone else stayed, too. When Vernon felt someone sitting down on the bed above him, he stuck his head out from beneath it. As luck would have it, his head came up right between Virgil's legs! From across the cell **Raucous** Rowdy Roddy spotted the snake and

Shouting

Loud

and went wild. He jumped up on his bed and started to dance around. With his hand over his mouth, he pointed at **Vacillating** Vernon.

Virgil bent over to look between his legs and met the snake, nose to nose! Vernon, not knowing what else to do, took this opportunity to lick **Vociferous** Virgil right in the face.

"Sluuuurrrppp!"

"Yeeech!" screeched Virgil as he jumped to his feet. Scared out of his wits, he ran over and tried to climb on top of Roddy.

Knowing that they had to be quiet to get out of jail, the two men silently hopped around their cell, waving their arms and pointing at the snake.

They tried to get the sheriff's attention without saying a word. They hung onto the bars of the door, but the only one paying attention was **Infamous** Amos!

"What are you two nuts up to?" he asked. "Cat got your tongue?" **Infamous** Amos laughed. Bugging these guys was going to be fun.

Then the big bad bully spotted Vernon. Amos shivered, his heart began to pound.

"A snake!" Amos gulped. Being tough was important to him. But snakes, snakes just plain scared him. He couldn't let anyone know that he, the meanest of the mean, was afraid of something so small. It would ruin his tough

reputation.

Infamous Amos continued his taunting.

"Sissies! Sissies!" he said. "It's just a poor little snake!"

When **Vacillating** Vernon heard what he thought were kind words about him coming from Amos, the 'poor little snake' decided to meet this wonderful new friend in the next cell.

With a flick of his tail rattling all the way, Vernon skedaddled across the floor.

"Maybe it's the slurping action that humans like about snakes," Vernon thought to himself, eager to test it out on Amos.

Sheriff **Rectitude** Dude and Judge **Venerable**

Vin Ho had neer seen a prisoner cry before. They were truly shocked to hear the sobs coming from the back of the jail. When they walked toward **Infamous** Amos' cell, they found him on top ofhis bed, clutching his blanket and begging the sheriff to save him!

Rectitude Dude spotted Vernon and calmly opened the door, expecting to grab the snake and remove the problem. But just as he got the cell door open, that big, tough, bully, **Infamous** Amos, jumped off his bed and into the arms of the sheriff. Surprised, the sheriff barely noticed when his ring of keys were knocked from his hand onto Vernon's tail!

Goodness

"Oh boy, another present from the humans! **Vacillating** Vernon exclaimed to himself.

Vociferous Virgil and **Raucous** Rowdy Roddy could not keep quiet any longer. They screamed to the tops of their lungs:

"SNAAAAAAAAAAAAKE!"

Scared by the loud noise and of what might happen next, because one can never trust a human who yells, Vernon decided to exit Inmate Inn, leaving **Infamous** Amos crying and clinging to the 'arms of the the law.'

Opening the front door, **Venerable** Vin Ho bowed to **Vacillating** Vernon as he crawled out, the keys jingling around his tail as he went.

The judge respected justice and the effect of this snake was evidently an appropriate punishment for such a scaredy-cat criminal. **Vociferous** Virgil, **Raucous** Roddy Roddy and especially **Infamous** Amos would not forget this experience. Of that he was sure.

Vacillating Vernon nodded his head humbly back at Judge **Venerable** Vin Ho. 'Justice at Inmate Inn' now had a whole new meaning. Proud of receiving respect from someone of such authority, Vernon held his head up high all the way back to his safe haven.

"I hope one of these keys will unlock **Variegated** Verna's heart," said the love-sick

snake. **Vacillating** Vernon slipped the sheriff's keys off his tail and dropped them next to the other treasures he had collected and hidden at the edge of the haystack at the end of the street in this funny human town called Fort Word, Texas.

SHERRIF
I

CHAPTER IX

exasperated
Vexed Tex

calming
Appeasing Polly

soothing
Mollifying Molly

A BUNCH OF HOPPING HUMANS!

Mollifying Molly placed her apple pie on the window sill to cool. It was a favorite of her husband's, and as a blacksmith, he had been extremely frustrated lately about the problems at his stable, Saddles and Spurs. Molly was sure that the apple pie would make him feel better.

Her daughter, **Appeasing** Polly, who was a pleasing child, packed an extra apple in her lunch pail for her teacher. Polly was always willing to help people too.

Earlier that morning, **Appeasing** Polly had climbed into the hayloft and out onto the roof of the stables. She hung the letter {S} where her papa had directed her to—at the highest point of the roof. Her papa's word that began with the letter {S} was a new one for her, but when she understood what it meant, she knew he had a good chance to win the contest.

Mollifying Molly sent her daughter off to school with a hug and a word of thanks for helping in the kitchen. While waving good-bye to **Appeasing** Polly, **Mollifying** Molly spotted a shabby old man coming toward the stables. It was **Polemical** Polecat leading his mule and he had a angry expression on his face.

"Oh, my!" Molly thought. "I hope Tex can deal with Polecat without adding to the frustrations of the day."

Earlier that morning **Bellicose**

Calming

Quarrelsome

Rose and **Belligerent** Brent, two hot-tempered sharpshooters, had already **vexed** her husband with their arguments over who was the best shot.

And now **Polemical** Polecat, who seemed to enjoy arguing, was bringing his mule in again. Maybe it was because he was a hermit and felt that arguing was the best way to conduct business. She didn't know.

Vexed Tex was in the stable stoking up the fire in his forge. His tools were neatly hung on the wall. Fresh straw had been spread on the ground and hay placed in the feedboxes for the horses that were to be shoed that day. Tex was upset because he was short on horseshoes, and he knew he would have to give up his lucky one that was hanging over the doorway. He was so busy that he did not see the rattlesnake moving silently under the hay.

But **Vacillating** Vernon was definitely watching **Vexed** Tex. He had gotten up early that Friday morning and scouted the whole town without incident. He was out before the humans, and when he saw the sparks that came from the blacksmith's fire, he was drawn to the stables. Vernon thought that if he watched closely enough, he could learn something here.

"You could learn something here, if only you would pay attention!" said an angry voice

Exasperated

that surprised Vernon. At first he thought someone was reading his mind, but soon realized that the voices came from the two gunslingers arguing out by the corral.

"You can't hit the broadside of anything!" argued **Bellicose** Rose, ready to get into a fight with her competitor.

"My not-so-fair lady, I most certainly would not agree with that statement," angrily responded **Belligerent** Brent, the Fighting Gent. "I am better than you and anyone else around!"

Well, if you are so good, then you must be able to hit flies off the tail of, hmmmmph, let's say, that there mule," **Bellicose** Rose said as she pointed at **Mawkish** Maude.

Maude raised her head when she heard her name.

"Don't mess with my mule, you ornery, no-good, low-down, no-count, backward, gun-totin' pair of confused pea-shooters," shouted **Polemical** Polecat, who considered name-calling an art, at which he was obviously the best.

Vexed Tex stepped out from the stables to break up the three.

"What can I do for you, Polecat?" asked Tex, trying to change the subject.

Quarrelsome

"Maudie here needs a new shoe on the back left leg. Lost it last week, and I want

it done in a hurry," answered the hermit as he petted **Mawkish** Maude on the top of her head. The mule spun her head around and stuck out her lips. **Polemical** Polecat was always in a bad mood, and his name-calling got him into many fights over nothing. But his mule loved him. She was constantly puckering her mouth as if she wanted a kiss. This was the only time **Polemical** Polecat would not argue. He gave her a big smack on those mule lips.

"Yuck!" thought Vernon as he watched the action from his hiding place beneath the hay.

Vexed Tex was frustrated because he knew he would have to take care of Maude before he could settle the argument between the sharpshooters. Polecat would have it no other way. So Tex tied her up, measured her back left hoof, and began to work on shoeing her.

Vernon turned his attention to the commotion outside the stables. He noticed that the two people carrying rifles were painting something on the top of the fence, and it didn't smell very good!

"If we put enough of this smelly stuff on top of the fence, the flies will come, and I will prove my point," argued **Belligerent** Brent.

"That smell is the best thing about you," **Bellicose** Rose replied, "but you didn't

Quarrelsome

Exasperated

get enough of the stuff!

"Well, you go inside the stalls and start scoopin' up some of that you know what," Brent told his opponent.

"Not unless you do it, too," responded Rose.

Vacillating Vernon listened to the heated argument. "Now, this might be worth watching," Vernon thought to himself as his eyes followed the two into the stables.

Meanwhile, **Vexed** Tex picked up his hammer and bent over, tapping away at Maude's hoof. He was using his last horseshoe, the lucky one from above the doorway. The luck must have worn off because **Mawkish** Maude swung her head around, puckered up her lips, and kissed the blacksmith right on his rear end!

Surprised by this gesture, Tex jumped, slinging everything into the air. His hammer flew across the stable and landed on the coal shovel sticking out of the fire. Hot coals were flipped up into the air. And what goes up, must come down—down—down!

A shower of hot sparks covered **Bellicose** Rose, **Belligerent** Brent, **Polemical** Polecat and Tex, who was now very **vexed**! Vernon thought it was a nice little dance the humans were doing throwing their arms up into the air and jiggling from side to side. Then, as he was just

Quarrelsome

beginning to enjoy himself, something came down around his neck with a thud. It was the lucky horseshoe!

"Huh?" Vernon said, in a surprised daze.

Leaving the bunch of hopping humans behind, Vernon started to drag his new good luck charm toward the boardwalk next to the haystack at the other end of the street.

He wondered if **Variegated** Verna would ever realize how lucky she would be to have him as a friend.

precise
Scrupulous Scarlett

CHAPTER X

extravagant
Lavish McTavish

BUT THAT HUMAN WAS NO INDIAN!

Exasperated

Vacillating Vernon was exhausted from dragging the horseshoe from **Vexed** Tex's Saddles and Spurs Stable all the way to the haystack. Crawling under the boardwalk was usually easy, but not now, not with a heavy piece of iron around his neck.

"I need a rest, and now would be a nice nap time," said Vernon as he heard the twelve rings of the church bell announcing noontime.

"The humans quiet down after they hear those bells. This would be a perfect time for me to catch up on my sleep," sighed Vernon as he coiled up into a heap.

Hilarious Precarious Prescott, H. P. P. for

short, ran down the boardwalk to his papa's office. He had forgotten his lunch pail again, and Miss **Didactic** Dorothy, his teacher, had given him only a few minutes to fetch it. What made H.P.P. so funny was his large cowboy hat and his oversized boots, now clomping against the boards on the walk above Vernon's head. **Vacillating** Vernon, grumbling about his disturbed nap, looked up through the cracks just in time to see H. P.P throw open the door to the office of McTavish's End-of-the-Trail Cattle Company. **Hilarious Precarious** Prescott ran into his father's office just in time to interrupt a conversation between **Lavish** McTavish and his unruly cattle

foreman, **Tumultuous** Thomas.

"Hi, Ma!" yelled H.P.P when he spotted his mother, **Scrupulous** Scarlett, sitting politely in the corner of the room arranging papers in precise piles on the table next to her.

"Forgot my grub," he continued as he picked up and balanced a lunch pail on his head.

"Not grub, H.P.P. Use the gentleman's term, my meal or sustenance," corrected his mother, "and don't carry it up there. Carry it by the handle at your side. Act proper."

"Yes, Ma!" said **Hilarious Precarious** Prescott, winking at his papa behind the desk while running out of the office. Forgetting to close the door,

H.P.P. skipped back to school, balancing himself on the edge of the boardwalk as he went.

"That boy is going to be the death of us yet," said **Lavish** McTavish as he leaned back in his luxurious leather chair, lighting his hand-carved smoking pipe with a match.

"Or the death of himself," answered **Tumultuous** Thomas. "Remember when he tried to walk across the cattle pens by stepping on the backs of those longhorns? Nearly turned my hair gray! Sure as lightning I thought he was a goner!"

Lavish McTavish puffed on his pipe and said, "Or the time he tried to paint their tails with red paint. That boy sure has put himself

Extravagant

into some dangerous situations."

Vacillating Vernon had heard the clomp, clomp, clomp of **Hilarious Precarious** Prescott's boots for the second time as he was heading back to the schoolhouse. Spotting the open door, Vernon decided that this was an opportunity too good to pass up. Besides, he smelled something unusual, smoke and sweetness mixed together.

Once Vernon had silently slithered into the Cattle Company Office, he noticed several different odors. Standing in front of the desk was a cowboy covered with dust. His clothes were in disorder, his chaps were on crooked, and his boots smelled of something awful. He was obviously disturbed about something as he spoke to a neatly-dressed man behind a huge desk.

Lavish McTavish, twisting the end of his handlebar mustache, looked handsome with his hair parted down the middle and slicked back with oil.

Looking around, Vernon understood the word 'lavish' because the office and Mr. McTavish himself were fine examples of the word.

Lavish McTavish had one fancy office. The rugs on his floor were from the Far East. His big, bold, shiny furniture was carved by the best craftsmen in the West. Even the vest and coat **Lavish** McTavish wore were elaborate:

Extravagant

a red and blue plaid with fine threads of gold woven into the material. And the pipe he was smoking was expensive as well, embossed in silver.

"It's that pipe that is putting out the sweet smoke," thought Vernon to himself as he listened in on the conversation.

"I can't handle those ornery-headed cattle by myself!" yelled **Tumultuous** Thomas, who was obviously upset.

Tumultuous Thomas was always in turmoil. He always saw the glass as being half-empty and never as half-full.

"Let's hire some more hands, then," answered

Lavish McTavish. "But **Stuporous** Stan is out because I heard he is all banged up and on crutches."

"And we don't need to hire those two slow pokes, **Laggard** Luke and **Slothful** Slim. They are good-for-nothing," replied **Tumultuous** Thomas. "We need someone who is on top of things."

"Excuse me, it's time for tea, gentlemen," interrupted **Scrupulous** Scarlett, as she rang a small bell. **Tumultuous** Thomas, usually stormy and boisterous, was quieted by the soft, eloquent voice of his boss' wife. McTavish 's wife had dedicated her life to doing what was right and proper.

Servile Nile, the McTavish's

manservant, entered the room carrying a silver tea tray filled with various types of breads, meats, and cheeses along with a teapot full of hot tea. Trying to win the approval of his employers, he was always one step ahead of their wishes and demands.

"Tea, Madam?" asked **Servile** Nile as he offered a cup to Mrs.McTavish.

"Thank you, Nile. Your attention to detail is to be commended," **Scrupulous** Scartlett responded in her well-mannered style.

Lavish McTavish took a plate of food from the servant.

"Thank you, Nile, and would you please serve

Thomas a plate as well?" he asked.

Tumultuous Thomas stood up and spoke before **Servile** Nile could serve him.

"Don't have time, Sir. Got some broncos to break this afternoon, and I had better get started," said Thomas, still obviously upset about not having enough help.

Stepping back from the desk, **Tumultuous** Thomas shook out his hat against his leg, stirring up dust into the air. He didn't see Vernon, and poor Vernon didn't see Thomas' spurs. But he felt them. He definitely felt them—on his tail!

Rattlesnakes are known for their hisses, and they scare many humans with a shake of

Stormy

their tails, but very few people have ever heard a rattlesnake scream. This was a first for everyone at the End-of-the-Trail Cattle Company. This was a first for Vernon!

Vacillating Vernon let out a sound that caused **Servile** Nile to drop the food tray and to climb up on top of his boss, **Lavish** McTavish, who dropped his pipe and the plate in his hands.

Scrupulous Scarlett, in proper and precise form, lifted her arm to her head and fainted.

Vernon, of course, was not a happy snake either. **Tumultuous** Thomas, who was agitated by the whole ordeal, started kicking at Vernon.

Anything that was close to Vernon, he kicked. Finally his boot caught Vernon in the gut and slung him through the doorway.

Like a storm out of control, the disorderly cowboy kept kicking everything in his way. A small stool, a box, the food tray, the teapot and several other items from the floor went flying out the doorway as well.

Poor **Vacillating** Vernon landed with a thud on the boardwalk's edge. He gasped and took a deep breath. He heard a thump next to him and spotted the silver pipe that held the sweet smoke. He quickly pulled himself and the pipe through the closest hole

Uncertain

in the boardwalk and lay very still. Vernon examined the odd sweet smell and took a deep breath. A sharp pain reminded him of where the boot had met his underside. He had heard about Indians exchanging peace pipes to soothe things over. But that human was no Indian, and this was not so peaceful a peace pipe!

Unsure about his latest human gift, he placed the shiny silver pipe in the hay with the other things for Verna. **Vacillating** Vernon was glad that **Variegated** Verna didn't smoke and that she was peaceful, but most of all, he was glad that she was sweet.

money-making
Mercenary Mary

Billy Blythe

ridiculous
Inane Chow Mein

Chapter
XI

master
Virtuoso Peso

TOUGH
STUFF!
TOUGH
STUFF!

Vernon slept all through the night and half of the next day. It was Saturday and he was exhausted from all that he had experienced in the last couple of days. It was late in the afternoon, and loud noises coming from down the street woke him up. **Vacillating** Vernon peered through the cracks of the boardwalk just as an odd-looking man walked by on his way to the saloon.

The man was dressed in overalls and a tattered hat. His whiskers reminded **Vacillating** Vernon of the scrub brush out on the high plains. When he started plucking the strings on a stick attached to an upside-down washtub, Vernon was amazed. **Virtuoso** Peso, the name of the scruffy-looking man, was a tub player. But his music wasn't scruffy, it was wonderful.

Mercenary Mary, the saloon owner always ready to make a buck or two, had hired **Virtuoso** Peso to play music outside on the boardwalk so that would-be customers would want to come into her saloon and spend money. Peso was an expert with his instrument, and his music did the trick. His melodies brought smiles to the faces of people passing by. It was those smiles as well as the laughter that he heard coming from inside the saloon that gave **Vacillating** Vernon enough courage to continue his hunt

Master

for the meaning of true friendship.

He thought he had spotted the answer with **Meager** Meagan and **Serene** Maureen at Sophie's hotel, but he did not get to stay long enough to find out for sure. Then the Sheriff, **Rectitude** Dude, seemed to be friends with the **Venerable** Vin Ho, but leaving the jail quickly was necessary. Anyway, he wanted to learn specifically about the boy-girl friendship stuff. The only boy-girl interaction he saw was between **Bellicose** Rose and **Belligerent** Brent, and that didn't sound like the type of friendship Vernon had in mind.

Vernon slipped under the swinging doors

belonging to **Mercenary** Mary's Saloon and Cafe. Because there were so many tables, chairs and barrels inside, Vernon had plenty of places to hide. He could easily watch the comings and goings of Mary's customers.

The first person who caught Vernon's attention was the jolly bartender, Billy **Blythe**. His easy-going laughter made Vernon feel good inside. Billy would slap his customers on the back and listen to their troubles. He even told the same jokes over and over, laughing at each one of them as if he told them for the first time.

Cheerful

At the end of Billy **Blythe**'s bar stood a bird cage containing a bird most unlike **Furtive**

Fernando. This bird had colorful feathers and a hooked beak.

Denigrating Nate was a talkative parrot abandoned by a sailor drifting through Fort Word the year before. Nate, although a pleasant-looking bird, had a nasty habit of insulting anyone who walked by.

When Nate was new to town, he insulted **Mercenary** Mary as she walked through the saloon wearing a brand-new dress. She was ready to throw the bird out for spouting the words, "It's pink! It stinks!"

But when her rough and rowdy customers spent more time and more money in her business because they found the insulting parrot entertaining, she decided to keep the bird and gave the cook the job of taking care of him.

"Viper varmint! Viper varmint!" shrieked **Denigrating** Nate when he spotted **Vacillating** Vernon slithering through the doorway.

Vernon, startled for a moment, quickly hid behind a barrel expecting the worse from the alarm that Nate had given about his presence. Much to his surprise, no one seemed to pay attention. Maybe it was because 'varmint' was a word that could be applied to anyone in the saloon on that day.

Vernon immediately spotted two shady-looking card sharks

Insulting

demanding service from the silly cook, Inane Chow Mein. With scowls on their faces, **Voracious Spacious** Van Dyke and his opponent in the card game, **Avarice** Maurice, were deeply involved in their greedy ways. They could not get enough money or food or anything that they set their desires on.

"More food," shouted **Voracious Spacious** Van Dyke, sporting a roomy long coat that looked big enough to hold several men.

"Comin', comin'," responded a short little man with a long pigtail and a big smile on his face.

When **Inane** Chow Mein entered the room carrying a tray of food, Vernon liked him immediately. He was so silly-looking. He wore a bowl for a hat and his clothes were on backwards. And when **Inane** Chow Mein walked backwards, people couldn't tell if he was coming or going!

Customers often laughed at **Inane** Chow Mein's ridiculous ways and then laughed harder when **Denigrating** Nate would say, "Stupid trick! Stupid trick!"

But today, even with a bowl upside down on his head, **Inane** Chow Mein could not make either of the greedy card players smile.

Vernon quietly observed **Voracious Spacious** Van Dyke. His coat, at first glance, seemed too big for him, and it was covered

with large pockets inside and out. But Van Dyke was not rotund. He was not fat enough to need such a spacious coat. Vernon, watching closely, noticed that the coat pockets seemed to be bulging with mysterious items. **Voracious Spacious** Van Dyke kept reaching inside to pull out more gold coins to plop on the table.

Vernon liked the way the coins rolled around on the table and fell nicely with a "plunk!" Vernon had the lucky silver coin from the bank; maybe a gold coin to match was what he needed for Verna.

Vacillating Vernon decided that because the coat had lots of room, he might be able to slip inside to take a look, and then come out without

Van Dyke ever knowing that he had been there in the first place. And that was exactly what Vernon did. He waited until there was a loud discussion over the poker game, and then he climbed up **Voracious Spacious** Van Dyke's leg and started his search for the valuables clinking around inside the coat.

Vernon, who knew immediately that he had made a mistake, was beginning to feel a little crowded and a little hot and lot frustrated because this was not as much fun as he thought it would be.

Vernon squirmed.

Van Dyke squirmed.

Vernon moved.

Van Dyke moved.

Then as if a bright light was turned on in that brain of his, **Voracious Spacious** Van Dyke began to howl.

"I'll be darn tootin', sure as shootin', something is lootin' my goods!" he shouted.

"Bad sport! Bad Sport!" **Denigrating** Nate commented as his head bobbed up and down with excitement.

"A SQUIRREL!" hollered **Voracious Spacious** Van Dyke as he pushed himself away from the table. "THERE IS A BLASTED SQUIRREL IN MY COAT TRYING TO GRAB MY VALUABLES!"

Not a generous person, **Avarice** Maurice, thinking only about his disturbed card game and the money that he was losing, jumped up, drew out his six-shooter, and announced that he would solve the problem.

"Van Dyke, open the coat, and I'll shoot the darn critter!" bragged Maurice, trying to act tough.

When Vernon managed to poke his head out of a pocket gasping for breath, **Avarice** Maurice, expecting to see a little fluffy squirrel, was thrown back by the sight of a snake. Maurice tripped backward over his own chair and the gun went off. The bullet ricocheted around the room, bouncing off several objects until it finally came back and hit the belt buckle of the would-be hero **Avarice** Maurice!

Greed

Now very mad and more determined, Maurice reached into Van Dyke's coat.

"Let me at that varmint!" he exclaimed.

"Viper varmint! Viper varmint!" echoed the insulting parrot, **Denigrating** Nate.

Maurice reached in and grabbed **Vacillating** Vernon by the neck, who was tangled up in the chain of Van Dyke's pocket watch. Maurice yanked, twisted and pulled on poor Vernon until the most interesting thing happened. **Avarice** Maurice, the mean, greedy **Avarice** Maurice, showed everyone what he was made of. Just as he thought he had all of Vernon and the pocket watch out of **Voracious Spacious** Van Dyke's coat, the greedy card player felt something happen. Because his belt buckle was broken, his pants became very loose and they

DROPPED TO THE FLOOR!

The room immediately went silent. Everyone was surprised at what they saw. The mean, nasty, greedy **Avarice** Maurice was standing in the middle of the room with his pants down! But more surprisingly, his underwear was showing. Showing lots of little bitty hearts and cute tiny angels.

Inane Chow Mein started to giggle. Then **Mercenary** Mary began to snicker. **Voracious Spacious** Van Dyke laughed so hard

that he fell down and rolled around the floor, coat and all. Billy **Blythe**, the bartender, knew that this incident would soon become the funny story to be told over and over.

Even **Virtuoso** Peso, who was playing his tub fiddle on the boardwalk, came inside the saloon to see what the noise was all about, and could not help but laugh at what he saw.

Avarice Maurice, who was very embarrassed, dropped Vernon and the pocket watch. With one hand he tried to cover himself up. With the other hand he picked up a handful of coins from the table top and threw them at the snake.

Vacillating Vernon wanted a gold coin but did not wait. He moved quickly, still wrapped up in the chain, dragging the pocket watch behind him. As he scrambled out the saloon doors, everyone in the room was laughing.

Everyone except Maurice.

"Tough! Stuff! Tough Stuff! AWWWWWK. Cute Stuff! Cute Stuff!"

Denigrating Nate said it all.

WANTED

One
Sturdy
Belt Buckle

As Soon As Possible!

LOVE AND PEACE

Euphonious Euphonia

Monotonous Mona

On Sunday morning, Vernon woke up early. He was ready for something a little calmer. The warm soft haystack was now his haven. He enjoyed the solitude from all the commotion that this town held. And he had gathered quite a collection of things, too. He wasn't too sure what he was going to do with them all. Had **Furtive** Fernando known that he would end up with this human stuff and that this stuff might win over **Variegated** Verna? He could use a friend right about now. Last night at the saloon was a nightmare he didn't want to repeat.

Vernon heard soft footsteps approaching and stuck his head out from under the hay. Three women in colorful flowing dresses with matching bonnets were walking towards the church. When they passed the haystack, one of the women dropped her handkerchief on the straw. As **Harmonious** Harriet reached down to retreat her hankie, she spotted something sticking up out of the hay. Vernon panicked for a moment wondering if he had misplaced one of his collectible items.

"Look, sisters!" exclaimed **Harmonious** Harriet as she held up the letter {F}. "I bet this is the missing letter for the schoohouse."

"Read the tag! Read the tag! Read the tag!" answered her sister, **Monotonous** Mona, who liked to repeat one sound over

Repetitious

and over.

The three sisters looked at the tag together. Sure enough, the letter was meant for the schoolhouse, and now they had found it. The third sister, **Euphonious** Euphelia took the letter {F} and started to sing in her beautiful voice,

"*Oh, boy! Oh, boy!*
What a joy! What a joy!
We'll deliver it today,
Won't Miss Dorothy be gay!
We'll see her after church.
A surprise awaits her thirst!"

"Wait a minute," responded **Harmonious** Harriet, "the word 'church' and 'thirst' are not sweet-sounding. You need to work on that part, 'cause as we all know, harmony is very important."

"Come on, come on, come on," urged **Monotonous** Mona. "We have to practice, practice, practice!"

The Sisters Three hurried on their way to Peaceful Word Chapel for their early morning choir practice.

After checking to see that all his possessions in the straw were safe and sound, **Vacillating** Vernon decided to follow the ladies.

"If someone is looking for a bit of peace as I am, what better place than a church," Vernon assured himself.

Repetitious

Vacillating Vernon slithered along under the boardwalk. It was still early, and the rest of the churchgoers were not up yet.

As Vernon got within earshot of the chapel, he heard beautiful music. The Sisters Three were rehearsing their special anthem for the service later that morning. The music sounded nice to his ears. **Euphonious** Euphelia sang like a songbird. She was known far and wide for her ability to hit the highest notes and make the sweetest sounds.

Her sister, **Harmonious** Harriet, was no slouch either. She skillfully and pleasantly combined her lower notes with her sister's.

Their duets were often featured in church services or at special town events.

Because **Monotonous** Mona, the third sister, could sing only in one tone, she was discouraged from singing, so she was given the job of playing the pump organ, a very important contribution.

Vernon listened carefully, trying to make out the words. They sounded very pleasant.

"*We've got love and peace,*

We've got joy and happiness,

We've got faith and trust."

"Hey," Vernon excitedly said to himself. "These are nice things to sing about. I have a strong feeling that I will enjoy this. My answer for

Repetitious

Variegated Verna might be here too, because they did mention love."

Searching for an entrance into the church, Vernon noticed that the two huge oak doors in the front were tightly closed. Looking on both sides of the building, Vernon saw that the stained-glass windows were closed.

"Now what am I supposed to do?" Vernon questioned as he began **vacillating** again. "Should I search another place? Stay here and wait? Go back to the haystack?"

At that moment a soft wind began to whistle through the bell tower above him, and he looked up.

"Hey! An opening!" he exclaimed. "I bet I can get in through there."

Vacillating Vernon easily slithered up the oak tree beside the church and out onto a branch. When he was level with the bell tower, he stretched his body over the chasm to the ledge on the building. He wasn't sure how he was going to get down into the church until he noticed that a thick rope was tied to the ball-shaped clapper inside the bell.

"All I have to do is to climb up under the bell and onto that ball and then down the rope," said **Vacillating** Vernon, proud that he had figured out the problem.

Uncertain

After Vernon crawled up under the bell and onto the round, cool clapper, he began to feel confident about his decision.

"This is going to be a breeze!" he announced to himself. But just as the words left his mouth, he felt a movement in the rope attached to the clapper. **Ethical** Ethelbert, the traveling parson, was about to ring the bell to announce the first call to church. Later he would ring it again announcing the beginning of the service, stopping only when everyone was inside.

Vernon immediately sensed a problem.

"I can't believe bad luck is happening to me again!" exclaimed Vernon as the bell began to ring. Back and forth the clapper hit the sides of the bell. Vernon held on for dear life. His head began to spin, and he saw bright stars appear before his eyes.

Thank goodness, **Ethical** Ethelbert only gave three tugs on the rope. After the parson left, Vernon slowly lowered himself down the rope to the floor. He was dizzy and his eyes were seeing things a little differently. Vernon noticed the end of the bell rope. It was coiled up on the floor like another snake and for a moment Vernon thought he must have made it into snake heaven!

Correct

Ethical Ethelbert believed in proper and correct conduct, in always doing the right and

moral thing. He decided that he should discuss with the Sisters Three the letter {P} given to him as his clue in the contest. He should not make this decision alone.

"If we win, we can share the prize with all the members of the church. That is the right thing to do," he told the sisters. "So we have to come up with a wonderful word that will win."

"{P} has to stand for peace," stated **Harmonious** Harriet, "Why else would you receive the letter {P}? Remember what it was like before we made peace with the Indians? Peace is truly valuable."

"But {P} could stand for lots of other valuable

things, too," interrupted **Monotonous** Mona, "like performance, performance, performance. Ours, to be exact. Or praise, praise, praise, that is an important valuable part of our church!"

"Or promises," chimed in **Euphonious** Euphelia. "God gave us promises, so promises are very special."

"You don't think it could be prosperity? Do you?" asked **Ethical** Ethelbert. "Most people would guess that value and prosperity go together. But I am leaning toward peace. Or praise. Or promises. Oh, this is too hard. Why don't you ladies practice your anthem one more time, and maybe we can decide together afterwards."

Musical

The music helped Vernon shake off his confusion from the bell-ringing incident. He crawled along in the shadows of the aisle. **Ethical** Ethelbert and the three lovely ladies were in the choir loft at the front of the church. One of the ladies was sitting in front of a large box. Vernon had never seen an organ before and went to investigate. Careful to remain as hidden as possible, he found cover under the front pew. The shiny white keys looked like something fun to touch. But because everyone was looking at the white papers on the music stand, he guessed that those papers might have answers to his question.

Startled by loud music from the box, Vernon began to feel the vibrations move up his spine.

Montonous Mona's feet pumped the pedals up and down, up and down, pushing air through the pipes. The organ began to shake a little and **Euphonious** Euphelia, along with her sister, **Harmonious** Harriet, sang the same song Vernon had heard before:

"*We've got love and peace,*

We've got joy and happiness,

We've got faith and trust."

Vernon was drawn toward the box. He couldn't help it. He wanted to feel more. He wanted to see how the box—

Compatible

"SNAAAAAAAAAAKE!" screamed Mona jumping up from her stool, her arms waving in the air.

Her sisters and Ethelbert immediately jumped up as well. One of the four humans knocked the music stand over, and it came crashing down with a loud noise, sheet music and hymnal books scattered everywhere.

Vacillating Vernon was immediately covered with sheet music. As if a sign from heaven, the two front church doors opened up. In walked **Mollifying** Molly and **Appeasing** Polly, who had come early to see if they could help in any way.

Quickly figuring out the problem, **Mollifying** Molly grabbed a poll hook used to open the higher windows in the church and gently prodded Vernon and the moving sheet music out the door. She remained calm. With **Appeasing** Polly's willing help she soothed the choir members.

Vacillating Vernon was just arriving back at his haystack when he heard the church bells ring again. He took a deep breath and gave thanks that he was not near that bell.

Placing the sheet music beside his other collected treasures, he noticed the title, '*Love and Peace.*'

"I need that," he said to himself. "I need that

Calming

A Lot!"

P
S

CHAPTER XIII

ashamed
Mortified Morty

indistinct
Nebulous Nick

risky
comical
H.P.P.

heartless
Callous Alice

EYE JEWELRY

calming
Appeasing Polly

unpredictable
Erratic Patrick

Didactic Dorothy, the enlightening and instructive schoolmarm, never passed up an opportunity to turn an event, a problem, or an incident into something educational for her students.

"A lesson is around every corner," she would say as she peered over her eyeglasses to make a point.

Most of the time her students would listen, even **Erratic** Patrick. His body was constantly on the move, and he usually listened with only one ear. But today **Didactic** Dorothy had all ten pairs of ears directed toward her. The news about the contest and the most valuable word was flowing like a gullywasher after a downpour.

Last Monday, the children had been saddened by the fact that their building was the only one in Fort Word that had not received a letter and a direct challenge to find the most valuable word for their town.

Now, with the discovery of the missing letter {F} by the Sisters Three, it was important that everyone settle down and help come up with a word that would be considered valuable.

Listening intently, **Appeasing** Polly, who brought an apple every day to please her teacher, was trying to calm the class.

"Shhhhhhh!" she said.

Listless Leslie, sluggish

Calming

from her early morning chores, tried not to slump.

Hilarious Precarious Prescott, on the other hand, was trying to distract everyone's attention again. He was balancing his pocket knife on his nose while crossing his eyes. Trying to be funny, he was always doing risky tricks, climbing to the top of the buildings and trees and such. Everyone remembers his comical attempt of painting the tails of the bulls at the cattle company red.

"Stop that, H.P.P.! Listen to Miss Dorothy," said Polly. Hilarious Precarious Prescott took the pocket knife off his nose and started balancing it on his fingers. His funny antics were not well received.

"StttttSTTTTTStttttSTTTop!" Nebulous Nick stuttered. His speech impairment usually made his words unclear and murky, but not this time. He wanted to hear about the contest, and he wanted no distractions.

Candid Candace once told Nebulous Nick that he had speech problems and should look into fixing them. Knowing her father could find a medical solution, she was straightforward with Nick, unlike the other children who snickered or ignored him completely.

Miss Didactic Dorothy started to sit down at her desk while addressing the

Indistinct

class. She failed to see the fake snake in the middle of her chair. She sat down and jumped up in one fell swoop. Seeing what she thought was a real snake, she grabbed it and slung it haphazardly across the room. The snake flew through the air, and lo and behold, it landed right in the lap of **Duplicity** Dusty, the trickster of the class who planted the fake reptile and then denied doing it.

"Now let this be a lesson to you," reprimanded Miss Dorothy as she grabbed **Duplicity** Dusty by the ear and sat him on the stool in the corner. The dunce cap was placed firmly upon his head.

The screams and hollers from Dusty followed

by the laughter of the schoolchildren drew the attention of **Vacillating** Vernon, who was trying to make up his mind where to go next on his quest for the answer to true love. He had gathered an egg, a feather pen, sticky candy, a towel, a pocket watch, sheet music, a set of shiny keys, a peace pipe, a silver coin, and a horseshoe to offer **Variegated** Verna as gifts. But **Vacillating** Vernon was still not sure if he had found the answer **Furtive** Fernando said could be found in the human town.

"How slow can I be?" he said to himself. "If you want to learn something, a school should be the place to find the answers."

Secretive

Vacillating Vernon slid up a trellis and into an open window at the back of the one-room schoolhouse. Lunch buckets were lined up in order under the neatly hung caps and bonnets belonging to the students. The smell of food in the lunch buckets made Vernon's mouth water. His distraction by the odor of food quickly ended when he heard the cold-hearted voice of a young girl, **Callous** Alice.

"Morty! Your clothes are all rumpled and full of holes," she said. "Don't your pa have enough money to buy some decent school clothes?"

Miss Dorothy corrected the heartless young girl. "Alice, we don't hurt people with words and we don't use bad grammar."

Mortified Morty's face turned red. He wanted to hide. He was embarrassed about most everything, but the condition of his attire was most embarrassing.

"Now," said Miss **Didactic** Dorothy, "Let's continue our studies about medieval times. I had planned to have you listen as I read a chapter from the book, *A Jester's Gesture*, but the contest for finding the most valuable word in Fort Word will soon be over."

The schoolmarm laid the book down on the desk and continued talking to her very attentive class. "We have been given a chance.

Ashamed

Dishonesty

You have all heard about the challenge to find the most valuable word. Well, it appears that our letter was lost in the shuffle, and we now have only until the arrival of the stagecoach at noon to come up with the solution. We have to put our thinking caps on, and not the one that Duplicity Dusty is wearing!"

Giggles and titters were followed by raised hands.

"Yes, Candace?" asked Miss Didactic Dorothy. "What is it?"

"To be honest, Miss Dorothy, that leaves us with very little time and the odds are against our coming up with the right word," stated

Candid Candace.

"You're just a party pooper!" said Callous Alice in her usual insensitive tone.

Erratic Patrick noticed a movement among the caps at the back of the room and fidgeted in his seat trying to get a better view.

"Patrick, sit still," Miss Dorothy instructed. "Now Alice, let's not be so unfeeling."

"Mmmmmmmmmmbbbbbrreeemmmemem,"

"Yes, Nick? Take a deep breath and start again. Take your time," said Miss Dorothy gently. "What do you want to say?"

Heartless

"Re-re-remember Miss Miss Dorothy, when y-y-you told us to always do our b-best,

Indistinct

no matter w-w-what?" stuttered Nebulous Nick.

"You're right, Nick," answered Miss Dorothy. "We can give it our best. We need a powerful and unique and important word that starts with {F}."

"Fun starts with {F}," exclaimed Hilarious Precarious Prescott. "I love fun!"

Erratic Patrick was bouncing his legs up and down. "I like fast," he said, "just like my legs!"

Appeasing Polly raised her hand then gave her answer. "Feelings begin with {F}, Miss Dorothy, and respecting one another's feelings would be a powerful thing to do."

"Oh, that doesn't make sense," Callous Alice

interrupted. "Cause the words 'fights' and 'floods' are powerful, and they start with {F}."

Miss Dorothy raised her hand for silence. **Erratic** Patrick kept fidgeting in his seat. The movement among the caps at the back of the room was too tempting to ignore.

"Patrick, what is the matter?" asked Miss **Didactic** Dorothy in a firm voice.

"Somethin' is in our stuff," he answered, pointing at the bonnets and lunch pails.

"It's just the wind a-comin' through the window," Miss Dorothy," yelled out one of the children.

"Listen, class. Remember the pretend snake that Dusty put in my seat? Well, he

Unpredictable

helped me come up with the word we need. Dusty, come here," she said gently.

Duplicity Dusty climbed down off the stool that stood in the corner. He removed the dunce cap and walked sheepishly toward his teacher.

"Dusty, even though you scared me, and what you did was not a nice thing to do, I forgive you," Miss **Didactic** Dorothy said with a smile on her face.

The class shouted their approval in unison. Their excitement made them oblivious to Vernon as he slipped toward the front of the room. A tear was in his eye. He was moved by the teacher and her words.

Duplicity Dusty was so happy that he flung his arms around his teacher's neck. But in his enthusiasm he knocked Miss Dorothy's eyeglasses off her face and onto...

"A SNAAAAAAAKE!" yelled Erratic Patrick, "A SNAAAAAAAAAAAAAKE!"

Patrick's arms waving every which way set the class into a panic.

"It's just one of Dusty's stupid jokes trying to scare us with a mean, nasty, ugly, fork-tongued, fake snake," added Callous Alice with her usual rude comments.

When Duplicity Dusty, who was obviously not faking about

Unpredictable

being scared, jumped into the arms of his teacher, the class knew that Vernon was real.

Miss Didactic Dorothy, just as scared, started dancing around the room. Because she lost her eyeglasses, she was having trouble seeing. Her spectacles had fallen from her face and had, surprisingly, landed on Vernon's face in the correct, upright position! The glasses fit over his eyes making his face look much bigger than normal to all the children. That frightened them!

The glasses made the children look much bigger than normal to Vernon, frightening him!

Then the church bells began to toll, announcing the coming of the stagecoach and the dangerous arrival of Perilous Pierre carrying the information about the contest!

The children were yelling, screaming, and jumping around; the church bells were ringing; and Miss Didactic Dorothy, not being able to see clearly, could not at that moment figure out what lesson could be learned from all of this.

Appeasing Polly, knowing how to smooth things over, ran to the door of the school and opened it. Then she took the broom from the corner of the room and swept Vernon out the door. Her mother had taught her what to do.

"Quick, H.P.P. Take the letter and climb on top of the school and hang it at the

highest point you can reach," directed Polly.

Once the snake was gone, the class began to calm down. Taking Miss Dorothy's hands, they led her outside and everyone watched as Hilarious Precarious Prescott climbed up to hang the letter {F} on the highest point of the schoolhouse. Standing on the roof and with everyone's attention, he bowed facing backwards, wiggling his backside to the children below. They laughed and clapped at the same time.

The rumbling sound of the stagecoach was approaching and Miss Didactic Dorothy, who was worried about their safety, ordered the children up on the boardwalk and told them to stay together.

"Head toward the haystack in front of the New News Newspaper office," she instructed them. "We will soon learn who the winner of the contest is."

After the children left, **Vacillating** Vernon decided that going to school was not all it had been cracked up to be. He did not like being swept out of the schoolhouse. His pride and his backside were a little bruised. He knew now that he could not go back to the haystack. All those humans were going to be there.

He had to go back to his home. He had to see if

Uncertain

Variegated Verna was okay.

"I have no gifts and no answers!" said Vernon angrily as he straightened the eyeglasses on his face. Disappointed, he headed back toward the plains on the outskirts of town.

"I still do not know what it takes to make a friendship work!" he said to himself. "That Furtive Fernando said that the answer was in the human town. I have been all over it, and I have looked everywhere! Those humans have grabbed, kicked, pushed, stomped and bruised me. My ears are ringing from the yelling and now, all I have to show for my effort is this eye jewelry!"

DUNCE
$a^2+b^2=c^2$
9
×9
81
(ATE ONE)
A JESTER'S GESTURE
F

instructive

repetitious

compatible

dangerous

CHAPTER XIV

correct

devouring
roomy

musical

filled

peak

ashamed

overflowing

TO FIND THE ANSWERS, JUST LOOK!

With all the letters hanging at the highest point of each building, excitement was in the air. It was time for the stagecoach to arrive. Everyone had gathered along the street. This time they hid their fear of **Perilous** Pierre's reckless driving. They were willing to risk being in harm's way. Everyone in Fort Word was ready to see if they had selected the correct word to win the prize.

Even General **Garrulous** Garrison and his calm daughter, **Serene** Maureen, had come to discover the answer to the puzzle.

Poor Private **Pinnacle**. He was left in the tower at the fort. Looking through his spyglass, he watched for the first signs of the stagecoach on the road leading into town. But every so often he would swing the glass around to watch his sweetheart, **Serene** Maureen, walking to town with her father.

When Private **Pinnacle** spotted the stagecoach, he raised the flag to signal to the people in town. Then he looked down at the town one more time to try to catch a glimpse of his ever calm and lovely Maureen. It was during this last glance when he gasped. He knew what the most valuable word was in Fort Word, Texas! He knew!

Frantic, Private **Pinnacle** tried to get the attention of the people down on the main street of town. Sitting in the highest point of

Peak

the fort, he waved the flag back and forth again. He could hear the crowd yell with excitement. They thought that he was signaling the arrival of the stagecoach. He couldn't get them to understand, to realize that he knew the answer!

Perilous Pierre raced his horses into town, his hat half over his eyes, the stagecoach bouncing back and forth. Then he did something unusual. He slowed down. Maybe this meant that someone was going to get off. Maybe someone with the prize. Was it gold? Or silver? Or the deed to a parcel of land? Just as everyone's hopes were rising, Pierre, with reins in his mouth, reached back and pushed a large bag off the top of his stagecoach as he turned the corner at the end of the street. His load landed on the well-positioned haystack.

"See y'all next week!" he yelled over his shoulder as he continued on his way.

Sheriff **Rectitude** Dude stepped forward and picked up the large bag. He opened it and found the usual mail that was to be delivered. When he reached deep within the bag, he felt a box and pulled it out. On the tag attached to the box was the greeting: "*To The Winner of the Contest.*"

"Well, this doesn't make sense," said **Bountiful** Bogart the banker. "Does it say who

the winner is?"

"Doesn't look like it," responded Rectitude Dude.

"Is there another box or letter addressed to us?" asked Parson Ethical Ethelbert. "Surely there are instructions somewhere!"

Rectitude Dude poured out the mailbag and, with the help of several of the townspeople, went through the mail piece by piece. Every piece of mail was handed to the intended receiver, but none seemed to be connected to the contest or the discovery of the recipient of the prize.

Private Pinnacle had watched the commotion, and he decided that he would leave his post and climb down from the highest point and go into town. He knew the answer, and since no one was playing attention to him, he would have to make the trip to convince the crowd.

Doc **Salve** Salvador and **Vexed** Tex suggested that the sheriff open the box, so the contents would reveal the winner. The crowd joined in on the request with a resounding "Yeah!"

The sheriff knew that it was against the law to open mail intended for someone else, and he wasn't too sure that this was the right thing to do.

"Why can't the Judge **Venerable** Vin Ho decide?" **Lavish** McTavish asked. "He is the one who determines the justice around here." Again the crowd supported the request, and

Extravagant

Venerable Vin Ho stepped forward to give his opinion. "I believe that because we do not know who this box is specifically addressed to, we can open it to see if there are any instructions inside it. Then we will just simply follow the instructions," said the wise and respected judge.

Sheriff **Rectitude** Dude began to open the package. The crowd was quiet with anticipation. Inside the box was a folded piece of paper which he opened and read in a loud voice:

"TO THE WINNER OF THE CONTEST,
YOUR ANSWER AND YOUR PRIZE ARE
RIGHT IN FRONT OF YOU,"
(signed)
ONE WHO KNOWS"

The crowd began to stir, looking around.

"The only thing right in front of us is that horrible haystack," complained **Mercenary** Mary.

"You don't think that the prize is hidden in the haystack, do you?" yelled a voice from the back of the crowd.

The people pressed forward, causing the sheriff to hold up his hand and in a firm voice he asked everyone to move back.

"I will handle this," he said, determined to guide the townspeople with integrity.

Then sheriff directed three boys, **Erratic** Patrick, **Hilarious Precarious** Prescott and **Mortified** Morty to climb into the haystack and

Ashamed

search for the unknown. Morty was too embarrassed and simply said, "No, thank you." But Erratic Patrick took the first leap followed by Prescott who dove into the hay through the air. Laughter arose, both from the sight of Hilarious Precarious Prescott's feet sticking out of the haystack and because everyone was a little nervous about the outcome.

Then Erratic Patrick yelled, "I found something, Sheriff!" About the same time Prescott yelled, "I found something, too!" Erratic Patrick held up something gold in color, and Hilarious Precarious Prescott came up with something black.

"Hey, those are my keys!" exclaimed the sheriff. "How in blue blazes did those get here? The last time I saw them that darn snake had them around his tail."

"And that is my missing lucky horseshoe," said **Vexed** Tex, "and the last time I saw it was around that snake's neck!"

The sheriff instructed the boys to return to the haystack.

Each missing item that **Vacillating** Vernon had hidden in the haystack brought a surprise response from the crowd.

"My prize egg!" exclaimed **Profuse** Priscilla.

"My pocket watch!" yelled

Overflowing

Devouring

Roomy

Voracious **Spacious** Van Dyke.

"The missing music,"

chimed in **Euphonious** Euphelia, **Harmonious** Harriet, and **Monotonous** Mona all at the same time. The crowd stood in amazement as the boys continued to dig through the haystack. **Mortified** Morty had overcome his embarrassment and, in the middle of the excitement, joined in, trying to help.

All the lost items that **Vacillating** Vernon had come in contact with were right where he left them: the candy from the doctor's office, the feather pen from the newspaper office, the pipe that **Lavish** McTavish had sorely missed, the towel from the hotel and the silver coin from the bank. By the time the last item was removed, the haystack had been leveled; it was evident that it held no additional prizes.

"My eyeglasses! What about my missing spectacles? That snake took those too!" cried Miss **Didactic** Dorothy.

"Ma'am, they do not appear to be here," responded the sheriff just as **Replete** Pete pointed out the obvious.

"There are plenty of things here, but none seem to be what a person might call a prize," Pete said. "The items are things we had before the contest even started."

Mercenary Mary interrupted, "Yeah! What are

Money-making

all these shenanigans going on here, and how come we still don't know who won? I want the money!"

A loud call from down the street got everyone's attention.

"I know the answer! I know the answer!" huffed and puffed Private Pinnacle as he stumbled toward the crowd. "I know the most valuable word."

"Speak up, Private, give us the answer. I order you to give these fine people the solution to this mess! It is important that we find out who the winner is so that we can get on with the business at hand. Speak up!" commanded

General Garrulous Garrison, using more than enough words.

"The answer is right in front of you," puffed Private Pinnacle finding it hard to breathe and talk at the same time.

"That's what the note said," complained Vexed Tex, who was getting more frustrated by the minute. "Tell us what you know."

The crowd responded in unison with yesses and nodding heads.

"Well, follow me then, and you will see for yourself," stated Private Pinnacle as he offered his arm to Serene Maureen, the only one in the crowd who seemed calm and collected.

The eager crowd followed the couple as they walked back up the hill toward the fort. When they reached the top, Private **Pinnacle** told everyone to turn around.

"To find the answer," he said with a big sigh, "just look!"

FORGIVENESS

PATIENCE

SINCERITY

ENDURANCE

NOTABLE

INSPIRATION

CHAPTER XV

WHERE TRUE VALUES LIE

At first no one saw it.

Then **Nebulous** Nick, who had always had trouble being understood, yelled out in a clear, distinct voice. "I see it!" he said pointing toward the town.

When the crowd began to grumble, **Mollifying** Molly tried to make things better.

"What is it, Honey?" she gently asked Nick.

"Th-th-th-there!" he said as he pointed to the buildings.

"Th-th-th-the letters!"

"Nick's right, folks," said Private **Pinnacle**, as he climbed up on a rock so that everyone could see him.

"Let me explain. I see the letter {F} on top

of the school. Miss Dorothy, what was the word that you and your children came up with?" he asked.

"Forgiveness," she said.

"The general store is right next to it with the letter {R}. What word did you come up with, Replete Pete?"

"Respect," he answered. "We should be overflowing with respect."

"Sheriff, what was yours?" Private Pinnacle continued.

"{I} stands for the word integrity," answered Rectitude Dude.

"The next building is the Cattle Company.

Goodness

"What word did you come up with, Mr. McTavish, for the letter {E}?" asked the private.

"Endurance. We all have to have endurance or we won't make it," replied **Lavish** McTavish.

"The New News Newspaper is next. Mr. Bradford, sir, what word does your letter {N} stand for?" asked Private **Pinnacle**.

Mr. **Brevity** Bradford surprised everyone by using more words than usual to answer. "Value is being worthy of notice, so notable is my choice," he said proudly.

"My building is next with the letter {D}," interrupted the doc. "We were taught in medical school that dependability is a virtue for all doctors to have."

Knowing that the saloon was next, everyone looked at Mercenary Mary expecting a word that had something to do with money, but were surprised when she stepped forward and said the word "Sincerity."

Private Pinnacle turned to Soporific Sophie. Her head was nodding. In spite of the excitement, it looked as if she was half asleep.

"What word, Sophie?" the private asked softly.

Sophie looked at everyone and proudly said, "My letter {H} stands for honesty."

Plentiful

Bountiful Bogart cleared his throat and announced that to make things work in

Correct investment banking, one must have inspiration. "That is my word, inspiration," he said.

Noticing that the letter {P} was hanging on the belfry of the Peaceful Word Chapel, the crowd looked over at Parson Ethical Ethelbert.

"I know how valuable peace is," he said to the crowd. "Our church is even named after that wonderful word. But the word selected for this contest is one I see very little of and one that would make this town better. My word is patience."

The crowd nodded their heads in agreement.

Vexed Tex was frustrated because his building with the letter {S} was the last in line.

He was the last to give his answer.

"I had trouble finding a word," he said to the crowd. "{S} is a letter on many words that I deal with day to day, shoes, stables, saddles. Those do not sound valuable to most. But when I see a rider coming in from a storm looking for help, I know that solace eases his loneliness, grief or discomfort. Solace is the word I consider the most valuable."

General **Garrulous** Garrison spoke up in a commanding voice. "Well, Private, if you know which letter, I mean, which word is the most valuable, give it to us now!"

Wordy

Private **Pinnacle** raised his hand and pointed to

the town. The crowd watched. First his hand was directed toward the school, and then it moved to the general store, then to the jail, then to the cattle company, next to the newspaper office, the doctor's office and the saloon. Down the street his hand pointed to each building, one right after the other. Next was the hotel, the bank, the church and then at the last, he pointed to the stables.

"Look not only at the letters," said Private Pinnacle. "But put them together in order. Nebulous Nick did it!"

"I-I-I-su-su-sure-sure-d-d-did!" Nick proudly added.

Following the Private's directions, Miss **Didactic** Dorothy spelled out loud the letters in order.

"F R I
E N D
S H I
P S."

"F-R-I-E-N-D-S-H-I-P-S spell friendships," announced Chief **Concise** Cochise.

"That's it! It was right in front of us the whole time. Fort Word, Texas, is overflowing with friendships," added **Replete** Pete.

"We are very lucky to have as many as we do," stated **Fortuitous** Louis.

"We shouldn't waste any, either," said **Squander** Squaw.

The crowd was filled with excitement.

Meager Meagan hugged her new friend, Serene Maureen.

Slothful Slim and Laggard Luke lazily leaned against each other and smiled.

"YOU'RE ALL MY FRIENDS!" yelled Raucous Rowdy Roddy.

"YEAH, ME TOO," echoed Vociferous Virgil in a loud voice.

Even Bellicose Rose and Belligerent Brent looked at each other, grimaced for a second, smiled, and then shook hands.

Venerable Vin Ho raised his hand, and the crowd quieted down out of respect for him.

"It appears that even though times are good, there have been times when they were not, but one thing is for sure. We have always been rich with friends," he said.

"Our prize is the answer, the many friendships we have!"

The people of Fort Word shouted their approval. They started to walk back to town smiling, shaking hands, and patting each other on the back.

The sheriff, **Rectitude** Dude, escorted **Mercenary** Mary and **Soporific** Sophie. **Ethical** Ethelbert counseled **Deleterious** Delbert about his problems.

Hurtful

Appeasing Polly and Mollifying Molly helped Stuporous Stan along. Billy Blythe and Inane Chow Mein laughed and slapped each other on the back. The children gathered around Miss Didactic Dorothy to give her a hug. When The Sisters Three began to sing, '*We've Got Love and Peace,*' Polemical Polecat, Virtuoso Peso, Rustic Rusty and Vexed Tex joined in.

There was mention of a celebration, a special day to be set aside each year, a special day to be designated as Friendship Day in Fort Word, Texas, a special day to remind all people where true values lie.

The slithering creature was the farthest thing from their human minds.

CATTLE CO.
JAIL
STORE
SCHOOL

D
SALOON
$
DOC
H
HOTEL
BANK
CHURCH
STABLES

uncertain
Vacillating Vernon

Variegated
multicolored
Verna

CHAPTER XVI

SEEING CLEARLY NOW!

"Well, what are ya so down in the mouth about?" **Furtive** Fernando asked **Vacillating** Vernon as he plopped down under the saguaro cactus.

"Don't talk to me," answered Vernon in a disappointed voice. "You were wrong. You were flat wrong about that human town."

Furtive Fernando took off the bandana that covered his face.

"How do you figure that?" asked Fernando as he dropped his bandana to the ground.

"All I wanted to do was find out what a true friendship was made of, and all I got was a bunch of bruises and scratches. And they took away all those things they gave me. I was going to give them to Verna and now I have nothing. Those humans can be nasty creatures!" Vernon said harshly.

Fernando removed his hat and placed it on a limb of the cactus.

"I have to disagree, friend. Your answer is plainer now than it has ever been," insisted **Furtive** Fernando.

Vacillating Vernon looked up at Fernando with a puzzled look on his face.

"These spectacles make you look different. You look bigger, clearer. Why are you not so secretive any more?" asked Vernon.

"I am trying to make a point," responded Furtive Fernando. "We often overlook the obvious. And we sometimes do not see what is right in front of us. Take the human town for instance. Did you watch those humans put their letters up on their buildings?"

"Yes," answered Vernon. "What does that show?"

"Well," said Furtive Fernando. "They did not even notice that their letters spelled 'friendship' until Private Pinnacle pointed it out. And he spotted it when he wasn't even trying to find the answer. The most valuable thing has always been right in front of them."

"Yes. And the most valuable thing that I want is a friendship with Verna," said Vernon. "We have already been through all this. What is your point?"

Furtive continued, "Vernon, you said you wanted to know what a friendship is made of, what makes it work, and what makes it last, right?"

"Right," said **Vacillating** Vernon.

"Well," added **Furtive** Fernando. "Every word that those humans selected as their valuable choice is what a friendship is made of. Spell friendship for me, Vernon. Look down at the human town. Start with the school's letter. It's first."

Vernon turned,

Secretive

looked down at Fort Word and frowned, remembering his ordeal with the broom at the school.

"{F}," Vernon said, a little disgusted.

"{F} stands for 'Forgiveness'," explained the bird. "True friends forgive each other."

"What's next?" asked **Furtive** Fernando.

"The letter {R}," said Vernon.

"{R} stands for 'Respect.' True friends respect each other. What's next?" continued the buzzard.

Vernon looked at the front of the jail.

"The letter {I}," he said.

"{I} stands for 'Integrity.' True friendships are always founded on integrity," Fernando said.

"The letter {E} is next," Vernon added. "What does {E} stand for?"

"{E} is for 'Endurance'," answered Furtive Fernando. "A true friendship will last, endure through the hard times as well as the good."

"{N} stood for Notable. Tell me the connection there," demanded Vernon.

"Notable is anything worthy or memorable. Friendships are," noted Furtive Fernando.

"Now I am beginning to see!" exclaimed Vernon. "Doc Salve Salvador said the letter {D} stood for Dependability. Friends need to be dependable. And Mercenary Mary said that {S} on her saloon stood for Sincerity. Friends have

sincerity between them," said Vacillating Vernon excitedly, now that he was beginning to understand.

Furtive Fernando continued. "Friends need honesty to survive. That is what {H} stands for and speaking of honesty, I have something to show you."

Vernon was glad that he was still wearing the spectacles. He watched as Furtive Fernando turned his back to him and began to squirm a little. A zipper sound was made, and then the bird began to remove his feathers as if they were a coat.

"Well I'll be darned!" exclaimed Vernon.

Furtive Fernando was no longer a buzzard. Out of the pile of buzzard feathers stepped a roadrunner!

"Vernon, close your mouth. My name is Rookie Roadrunner, and it's time to be honest with you," he said.

"What do you mean?" asked Vernon, confused by the whole ordeal.

"Well, the next letter is {I} for 'Inspiration.' I need to not only be honest with you as a true friend, but I also need to inspire you to be the best friend you can be," answered Rookie Roadrunner.

Vernon closed his mouth and swallowed the lump in

Starter

his throat. He began to demand an explanation. The roadrunner stopped him.

"Before you ask anything, I have to remind you of the {P} word, Patience. Patience with your friends is required, me included. And when they need something, like you did, we need to offer them Solace, the word for the letter {S} on the stables," continued the roadrunner.

Vacillating Vernon, instead of shaking the rattle on his tail, shook his head in amazement. When he began to calm down, he asked. "Do you mean you are my friend? A true friend?

Rookie Roadrunner fluffed up his feathers and said, "Yes, I am. I always have been."

"Then answer two questions for me," asked Vernon. "Why the **Furtive** Fernando disguise?"

"Well, you see, partner," answered **Rookie** Roadrunner with a smile. "I am the mascot for the stagecoach company called the Roadrunner Express. But I am just a starter, a **rookie**. That's the reason for my name. As a **rookie**, I am given all the strange jobs and you must admit, sitting up here in the hot sun, checking on **Perilous** Pierre's deliveries is pretty strange. Some of those humans collect roadrunner feathers, so I figure no one would bother a buzzard. That reminds me: I am required to report in, so I've got to go."

Rookie Roadrunner began

to pick up his costume as Vernon started shaking his head back and forth again in amazement.

"Now, what was the other question?" asked Rookie Roadrunner.

"I don't know the meaning of the word 'Solace'," Vernon said. "I understand all the other words and how they are a part of a true friendship. But I don't know what the word 'Solace' means."

"I do," interrupted a sweet voice.

Vernon and Rookie quickly turned around. There was Variegated Verna in all her splendor. Her colorful skin shimmered in the light. Vernon's heart began to pound.

"Solace is an easing of discomfort and loneliness," said Verna. "Everyone needs a friend who can ease loneliness. And I have been lonely for a long time."

Vernon felt a new lump in his throat.

Variegated Verna moved closer to Vernon. "Do you know where I can go to find an answer to my problem?"

"Funny that you ask that question," replied **Rookie** Roadrunner. "My friend here, Vernon, has just come back from the human town, and I am sure he now knows all the answers to all the questions you might have."

Verna moved even closer to Vernon and winked.

"I like that eye jewelry," Variegated Verna said.

"I like what I see through this eye jewelry," Vacillating Vernon replied with a sheepish smile.

"I think I am going to be sick!" groaned Rookie Roadrunner. "Why don't you two friends just run along. I'm sure you have a lot to talk about."

As Vacillating Vernon and Variegated Verna began to crawl off through the brush and cacti, Vernon yelled back over his shoulder, "Thanks Furtive—I mean Rookie. I see things clearly now!"

Rookie Roadrunner took a deep breath, watched the two snakes slither off into the sunset and silently congratulated himself on a job well done. He waited until Vernon and Verna were a good distance away. Then he cautiously looked to his left and then to his right. He quickly stepped behind the saguaro cactus.

No one heard the sound of another zipper being unzipped. No one saw the roadrunner costume fall to the ground. And no one knew that something **furtive** was beginning to take a new shape on the flats outside of Fort Word, Texas.

"I'm going to have to work on that honesty thing!" said a sweet little voice.

THE END
Or is it?

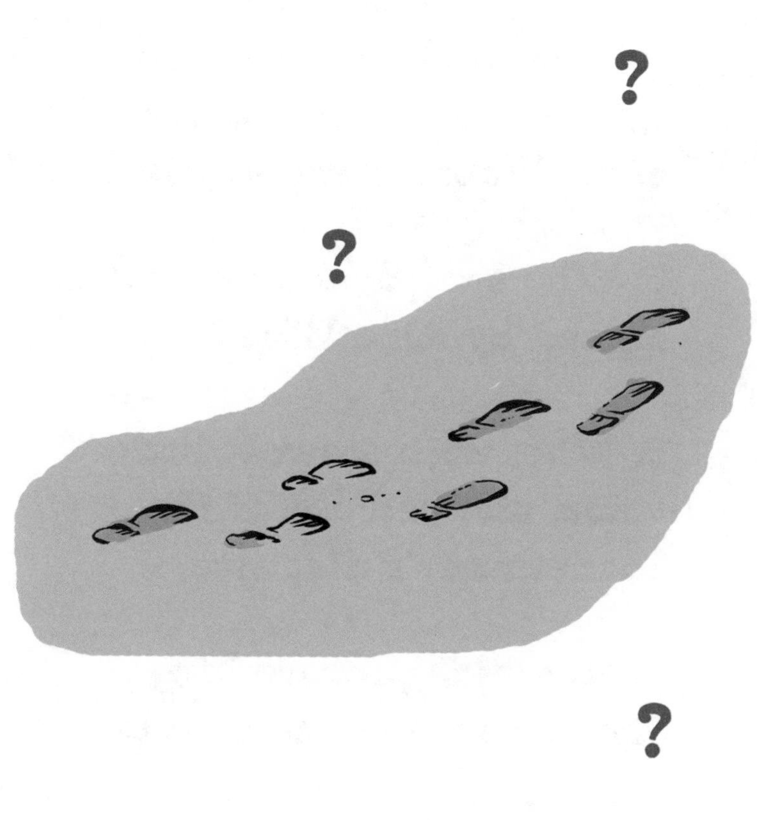

Conundrums

1. Which two characters have names that are opposite of their real personalities?

2. Who sent the contest letter signed by 'One Who Knows'?

3. Who, with a sweet little voice, stepped out of the roadrunner's disguise?

4. In which picture is a character without a name?

E-mail your answers to msmac@fortword.com

Lexicon

Test your memory.

Turn the page and see how many names of the characters from Fort Word you can remember.

Write them down.

Check your answers against the list at the end.

See the chart for a score.

Good Luck!

adjective

Appeasing

(uh **peas** zing)

Synonyms: willing, **calming**, yielding, peaceable, disarming

Antonyms: bellicose, fighting, aggressive

noun

Avarice

(av uh riss)

Synonyms: **greed**, penny-pincher, stinginess

Antonyms: charity, generosity

adjective

Bellicose

(**bell** luh cos)

Synonyms: quarrelsome, fighting, warlike, attacking

Antonyms: calm, easygoing, peaceful

adjective

Belligerent

(buh **lij** jer rent)

Synonyms: **quarrelsome**, fighting, aggressive

Antonyms: kind, nice, peaceful

adjective

Blithe

(bl-**eye**-th)

Synonyms: **cheerful**, jolly, merry, sunny

Antonyms: sad, depressed, miserable, unhappy

adjective

Bountiful

(**bown** tea full)

Synonyms: **plentiful**, ample, exuberant, galore

Antonyms: lacking, sparse, scant

noun

Brevity

(**brev** uh tee)

Synonyms: **shortened**, conciseness, curtness, brief, terse

Antonyms: lengthiness, wordiness

adjective

Callous

(cal luss)

Synonyms: **heartless**, careless, tough, unfeeling

Antonyms: caring, kind, sensitive

adjective

Candid

(**can** did)

Synonyms: **truthful**, blunt, straightforward

Antonyms: deceitful, tricky, insincere

adjective

Concise

(con s-eye-ss)

Synonyms: **brief**, compact, boiled-down

Antonyms: wordy, long-winded, verbose

adjective

Deleterious

(dell luh **tirry** us)

Synonyms: **hurtful**, damaging, injurious, bad

Antonyms: helpful, beneficial, aiding

adjective

Denigrating

(**den** uh great ting)

Synonyms: abusive, maligning, slanderous, insulting

Antonyms: complimentary, praising, flattering

adjective

Didactic

(die **dack** tick)

Synonyms: **instructive**, teacherly, academic

Antonyms: uninstructional

noun

Duplicity

(do **pliss** uh tea)

Synonyms: dirty trick, falsehood, **dishonesty**

Antonyms: honesty, loyalty, straightforwardness

adjective

Enervated

(**in** er vay ted)

Synonyms: **tired**, listless, run-down, worn-out

Antonyms: energized, activated

adjective

Erratic

(ih **rat** tick)

Synonyms: **unpredictable**, unstable, shifting

Antonyms: steady, predictable, unchanging

adjective

Ethical

(**eth** ick cull)

Synonyms: **correct**, good, honest, righteous

Antonyms: corrupt, dishonest

adjective

Euphonious

(you **fon** ee us)

Synonyms: **musical**, tuneful, melodic, soothing, smooth

Antonyms: ugly, cacophonous

adjective

Expeditious

(x puh dish us)

Synonyms: quick, hasty, rapid, effective

Antonyms: slothful, sluggish, slow, inefficient

adjective

Fortuitous

(four **two** it tus)

<u>Synonyms</u>: **lucky**, fortunate, accidental, chance

<u>Antonyms</u>: unlucky, predictable

adjective

Furtive

(fur tiv)

Synonyms: **secretive**, undercover, disguised, sneaky, sly

Antonyms: aboveboard, open

adjective

Garrulous

(gair uh luss)

Synonyms: **wordy**, motormouth, chattering, verbose

Antonyms: concise, taciturn

adjective

Harmonious

(har **moan** ee us)

Synonyms: **compatible**, musical, matching, melodic

Antonyms: mismatched, incompatible

adjective

Hilarious

(hill **air** ee us)

Synonyms: **comical**, laughable, amusing, entertaining

Antonyms: sad, serious

adjective

Humble

(**humm** bull)

Synonyms: respectful, shy, **modest**, meek

Antonyms: overbearing, bold, confident

adjective

Inane

(**in** ane)

Synonyms: **ridiculous**, trivial, silly, pointless, idiotic

Antonyms: sensible, intelligent

adjective

Infamous

(in fuh muss)

<u>Synonyms</u>: **rotten**, corrupt, hateful, vicious

<u>Antonyms</u>: reputable, noble

adjective

Laggard

(**lag** erd)

Synonyms: slow, **sluggish**, time-wasting

Antonyms: hard-working, prompt, on-time

adjective

Lavish

(lav ish)

Synonyms: **extravagant**, grand, luxurious, posh

Antonyms: meager, lacking, sparse

adjective

Listless

(**list** luss)

<u>Synonyms</u>: **lifeless**, slow, torpid, enervated, limp

<u>Antonyms</u>: energetic, lively

adjective

Mawkish

(maw kish)

Synonyms: sugary, mushy, sentimental, gooey

Antonyms: unsentimental, dry

adjective

Meager

(me gurr)

Synonyms: **not enough**, scarce, wanting, austere

Antonyms: enough, excessive, profuse

adjective

Mercenary

(**murr** suh nair ee)

Synonyms: **money-making**, greedy, materialistic, avaricious

Antonyms: charitable, not-for-profit

adjective

Mollifying

(mall uh fie ing)

Synonyms: **soothing**, quiet, willing, calm

Antonyms: harsh, aggressive, bitter

adjective

Monotonous

(muh **not** en nuss)

Synonyms: **repetitious**, toneless, unchanging, soporific

Antonyms: interesting, varied

adjective

Mortified

(**more** tuh fide)

Synonyms: **ashamed**, humiliated, rattled, embarrassed

Antonyms: confident, proud, relaxed

adjective

Nebulous

(**neb** you luss)

Synonyms: **indistinct**, indefinite, incoherent, murky

Antonyms: clear, well-defined

adjective

Perilous

(**pear** uh luss)

Synonyms: **dangerous**, hazardous, risky

Antonyms: safe, secure

noun

Pinnacle

(**pin** uh cull)

Synonyms: tower, **peak**, highness, summit

Antonyms: bottom, base, low point

adjective

Polemical

(puh **lim** ick call)

Synonyms: **quarrelsome**, cantankerous

Antonyms: agreeable, peaceful, tranquil

adjective

Precarious

(pruh **care** ee us)

Synonyms: chancy, **risky**, unpredictable

Antonyms: certain, safe, sure

adjective

Profuse

(pro **fewss**)

Synonyms: excessive, bountiful, **overflowing**, plentiful

Antonyms: meager, sparse

adjective

Prudent

(**proo** dent)

Synonyms: **sensible**, reasonable, advisable, wise

Antonyms: imprudent, unwise

adjective

Raucous

(raw cuss)

Synonyms: **loud**, unharmonious, blaring, ear-piercing

Antonyms: quiet, soft

noun

Rectitude

(**wreck** tuh tood)

Synonyms: **goodness**, decency, morality, integrity

Antonyms: corruptness, evil

adjective

Replete

(**ree** pleet)

Synonyms: **filled**, well-stocked, crowded, jammed

Antonyms: empty, lacking, meager

noun

Rookie

(rook key)

Synonyms: **starter**, tenderfoot, learner

Antonyms: expert, master

adjective

Rotund

(ro tund)

Synonyms: fat, husky, chunky, tubby, hefty

Antonyms: bony, skinny, slim

qdjective

Rowdy

(**rr ow** dee)

Synonyms: **wild**, loud, lawless, turbulent

Antonyms: peaceful, restrained

adjective

Rustic

(**russ** tick)

<u>Synonyms</u>: **country**, natural, rural, simple, unpolished

<u>Antonyms</u>: urban, sophisticated

verb

Salve

(sav)

<u>Synonyms</u>: soothe, mend, relieve, **make healthy**

<u>Antonyms</u>: aggravate, irritate

adjective

Scrupulous

(**screw** pew luss)

Synonyms: **precise**, moral, upright, strict, fussy

Antonyms: careless, slapdash, casual

adjective

Serene

(suh **reen**)

Synonyms: peaceful, undisturbed, **quiet**

Antonyms: agitated, nervous

adjective

Servile

(sir vile)

<u>Synonyms</u>: humble, **bootlicking**, slavish, groveling

<u>Antonyms</u>: bossy, assertive

adjective

Slothful

(**sloth** full)

Synonyms: **slow**, boring, lifeless
sluggish, listless

Antonyms: excited, lively

adjective

Soporific

(soap or **riff** ick)

<u>Synonyms</u>: **drowsy**, hypnotic, tranquilizing, snoozy

<u>Antonyms</u>: alert, invigorating, awake, energetic

adjective

Spacious

(spay shuss)

<u>Synonyms</u>: **roomy**, large, immense, cavernous, huge

<u>Antonyms</u>: pint-sized, confined, tiny

verb

Squander

(sk **wand** der)

Synonyms: to **waste**, use up, fritter away

Antonyms: make good use of, manage, save

adjective

Stuporous

(**stew** por us)

Synonyms: **dazed**, dizzy, unclear, uncertain

Antonyms: clear, responsive

adjective

Tumultuous

(two **mull** chew us)

Synonyms: **stormy**, excited, raucous, rowdy

Antonyms: calm, orderly, peaceful

adjective

Vacillating

(**vass** uh **late** ting)

Synonyms: **uncertain**, doubting, wavering, hesitant

Antonyms: certain, decisive, unwavering, sure

adjective

Variegated

(**vair** uh **gate** ted)

Synonyms: **multicolored**, showy, spotted, motley

Antonyms: plain, uniform, same, consistent

adjective

Venerable

(**vin** err uh bull)

Synonyms: revered, dignified, **honored**, wise

Antonyms: unrespected, lowly, undignified

adjective

Vexed

(vex t)

Synonyms: **exasperated**, fed up, disturbed, fretful

Antonyms: content, happy, satisfied, pleased

noun

Virtuoso

(verr chew **oh** so)

Synonyms: **master**, star, artist, maestro, hotshot

Antonyms: amateur, rookie

adjective

Vociferous

(voh **siff** err us)

Synonyms: **shouting**, noisy, loud-mouthed

Antonyms: quiet, silent

adjective

Voracious

(voh **ray** shuss)

Synonyms: devouring, mercenary, close-fisted, starved

Antonyms: quenched, satisfied, generous

Answers

1. Polly
2. Maurice
3. Rose
4. Brent, the Gent
5. Billy
6. Bogart
7. Bradford
8. Alice
9. Candace
10. Chief Cochise
11. Delbert
12. Nate
13. Dorothy
14. Dusty
15. Ernie
16. Patrick
17. Ethelbert
18. Euphelia
19. Ezra
20. Louis
21. Fernando
22. General Garrison
23. Harriet
24. Prescott
25. Trumble
26. Chow Mein
27. Amos
28. Luke
29. McTavish
30. Leslie
31. Maude
32. Meagan
33. Mary
34. Molly
35. Mona
36. Morty
37. Nick
38. Pierre
39. Private
40. Polecat
41. Prescott
42. Priscilla
43. Prudence
44. Rowdy
45. Dude
46. Pete
47. Roadrunner
48. Ruby
49. Roddy
50. Rusty
51. Salvador
52. Scarlett
53. Maureen
54. Nile
55. Slim
56. Sophie
57. Van Dyke
58. Squaw
59. Stan
60. Thomas
61. Vernon
62. Verna
63. Vin Ho
64. Tex
65. Peso
66. Virgil
67. Van Dyke

Look at What I Did!

I remembered **1-20 names**
- my brain is as warm as
Laggard Luke's bath water

I remembered **21-34 names**
-my brain is as sweet
as a Mawkish Maude kiss

I remembered **35-47 names**
-my brain is as bountiful as
one of Bogart's investments

I remembered **48-60 names**
- my brain is sizzling like
Vexed Tex's branding iron

I remembered **61-67 names**
-my brain is at its peak,
just like Private Pinnacle

noun

Friendship

(fr end ship)

Paste a Photo or Draw a Picture of
You And Your Closest Friend

Definition: a relationship built on forgiveness, respect, integrity, endurance, notability, dependability, sincerity, honesty, inspiration, patience and solace.

Date________